VERUM

VERUM

Book two in the *NOCTE Trilogy*

By Courtney Cole

The truth shall set you free.

***

Verum

Latin;

Noun; true
Adverb; in truth

Lakehouse Press, Inc.

This book is an original publication of Lakehouse Press, Inc.
All rights reserved.

Copyright © 2014, Courtney Cole
Cover Design by The Cover Lure (Matthew Phillips)

Library of Congress Cataloging-in-publication data

Cole, Courtney
NOCTE/Courtney Cole/Lakehouse Press Inc/Trade pbk ed

ISBN 13: 978-0692375242
ISNB 10: 0692375244

Printed in the United States of America

Dedication

To Natasha.
Because you always believe in me,
even when I don't.

Foreword

Dante Alighieri said, in his *Inferno*:
"Do not be afraid; our fate
cannot be taken from us; it is a gift."

Dante lied.

Our fate must be worked for.
It must be paid for.
With tears.
With blood.
With everything we have.

And it is not until the end,
the very end,
that we will know if it was worth it.

Prologue

"See you later, Cal. Are you sure you don't want to go?"

I look up from what I'm doing to see my brother in the salon door.

"I'm sure," I answer quickly. "I need some time alone. Go ahead and meet your friend."

"He had to cancel," Finn scowls. "So I guess I've been stood up. Are you sure you don't want to come?"

I groan internally because I'm not a fan of Quid Pro Quo, but Finn has been looking forward to this concert for months. There's no way I can really say no.

But then my mom walks in and rescues me.

"I'll go," she volunteers, and Finn crows.

"Sa-weet!" He glances over at me. "You snooze, you lose, Cal. We're blowing this joint."

I have to smile a bit as they walk away because this one small thing makes him so happy, because most guys our age would never go to a concert with their mom. But Finn isn't most guys.

I sink into the window seat, leaning my head against the glass as I watch their tail-lights disappear down the driveway.

Sweet Finn.

Especially now, after what Dare told me...after his confession, I need my brother.

Finn and I can't be separated. I know that more now than ever. We have to protect each other. We have to keep each other sane.

I pick up the phone.

Mom has to know, and it'll be late when they get home, so this can't wait.

But mom doesn't want to hear it right now. And then she screams.

Loud and shrill, in my ear.

"Mom?" I ask, the dread curling around my spine with icy fingers.

There's no answer.

"Mom!" I demand, scared now.

But there's still no answer.

Everything swirls around me, pictures and smells and sounds, and somehow, I know she'll never answer me again. In my mind, I see her face, and it's bloody and battered.

I can't breathe and I know in my heart she's gone as I race out to the porch, as I stare at the smoke winding its way into the night sky, just a little ways down the mountain.

I know it as I sink to a heap on the steps, gripping the phone.

I know it as nausea overtakes me in jagged waves and the world spins.

I know it as Dare limps across the lawn, his forehead bloody.

I know it as he stands in front of me, battered and raw.

"Calla, are you ok?" he whispers, his hand on my shoulder.

There's blood on his fingers.

"Are you ok?" he repeats.

I somehow manage to move my head, to look up at the man I love, the man I hate, the man I'm afraid of. Through it all, through all of the blood and the smoke, I can only concentrate on one thing.

One question.

"Why are you here?" I ask him stiltedly. "This doesn't make any sense."

"You know why, Cal." A drop of blood drips from his forehead.

Do I?

Suddenly, I don't know anything.

Nothing makes sense anymore.

My thoughts are jagged pieces.

"Where's Finn?" my lips move.

Dare stares at me, his dark eyes guarded and urgent.

"We've got to call an ambulance."

I'm frozen, so Dare grabs my phone and punches at the numbers.

His voice blends into the night as he speaks to the dispatcher, but one phrase penetrates the fog of my consciousness.

"There's been an accident."

I wait for him to finish, I wait until he hangs up and stares down at me before I finally speak.

"Was it?" I ask him, my voice shaking and frail and thin. "Was it an accident?"

He closes his eyes.

Chapter One

Everything is in slow motion.

The waves, Dare's mouth moving, his words. I stare at him, at the dark stubble on his jaw, at the way he swallows. At the way his dark eyes are impaling me, holding me, scaring me.

"You've got one question left, Calla," he reminds me now. "Ask it."

The past year swirls through my mind in blurs and snippets. Through everything, Dare has been here. He's been with me, he's held me, he's loved me.

Or has he?

My lips tremble as I try to move them.

"Why were you there that night?" I finally ask, choosing my words carefully. "You weren't supposed to be. But you were."

Dare answers my question with one of his own, staring at me cautiously.

"Which night, Calla?"

I'm speechless as I stare at him.

"You know which night. *The night.* The night my brother died."

Something wavers in Dare's gaze, but he gathers himself.

"Do you remember now? Do you remember how bloody I was?"

I'm already shaking my head from side to side, slowly, in shock. Not because I don't remember, but because I don't want to.

"There was a lot of blood," I recall, thinking about the way it'd streaked down Dare's temple and dripped onto his shirt. It'd stained the t-shirt crimson, spreading in a terrifying pool across his chest. "I didn't know if it was yours or... Finn's."

And for one scant second, I had forgotten that Dare had confessed something to me.

I'd forgotten that I was terrified of him because of it.

Because amid all of that blood, all I could see was my fear of losing him, because heaven help me, I loved him anyway.

"You held me up," my lips tremble. "When I was falling down. You held me while I waited for... Finn."

I'd waited for Finn to call.

I'd waited and waited and waited.

The sirens wailed in the night, and I'd paced the floor.

Finn never called.

Dare nods. "I've always held you up, Cal."

"When my father came in, and said... when he told me about Finn, everything else faded away," I recall, staring out at the ocean. *God, why does the ocean make me feel so small?* "Nothing else mattered. Nothing but him. You faded away, Dare."

The truth is stark.

The truth is hurtful.

I lay it out there, like flesh flayed open, like pink muscle, like blood.

Dare closes his eyes, his gleaming black eyes.

"I know," he says softly. "You didn't remember me. For months."

We know that. We both know that. It's why we're here, standing on the edge of the ocean, trying to retrieve my mind. It's been out to sea for too long, absent from me, floundering.

I snatch at it now with frantic fingers, trying to draw all of my memories back. They're stubborn though, my memories. They won't all come.

But one does.

My eyes burn as I fix my gaze on Dare.

"You confessed something to me. It scared me."

Dare's lids are heavy and hooded, probably from the weight of guilt.

He nods. One curt, short movement.

"Do you remember what I told you?"

He's silent, his gaze tied to mine, burning me.

I flip through my memories, fast, fast, faster... but I come up empty-handed. I only emerge with a feeling.

Fear.

Dare sees it in my eyes and looks away.

"I tried to tell you, Cal," he says, almost pleading. "You just didn't understand."

His voice trails off and my heart seems to stop beating.

"I didn't understand what?" I ask stiltedly. *Just tell me.*

He lifts his head now.

"It isn't hard to understand," he says simply. "If you remember all that I told you. Can you try?"

I stare at him numbly. "I've tried already. I... it's not there, Dare."

Dare's head drops the tiniest bit, almost imperceptibly, but I see it. He's discouraged, disappointed.

He shakes his head. "It *is* there. Just relax, Calla. It will come. But you should know now that you're not safe. You have to trust me."

"You were here for me," I tell him. "I remember that much. You were here for me all along."

Dare shakes his head. "No. That's not true. I came here for a reason, then that reason changed and *it was you.* I swear on my mother's life."

"Your mother is dead," I point out starkly. "And so is mine. And I'm supposed to just believe you now?"

Dare sighs, a ragged and broken sound. He tries to touch my hand, but I yank it away. He doesn't get to touch me. Not anymore.

"You don't understand," he says quietly.

I stare at him. "No, I don't." *And you have no idea what this feels like.*

"You will," he replies tiredly. "I swear to God you will."

A lump lodges itself in my throat as the sea breeze rustles my hair. I take a deep gulp of it, filling my lungs with the clean scent.

"Did you ever love me at all?" I ask, the words choking me, because no matter what, it's the most important thing to me right now.

Pain flashes across Dare's face, real pain, and I brace myself.

Don't.

Don't.

Don't.

Don't hurt me.

"Of course I did," he says quickly and firmly. "And I do still. Right now."

He stares at me imploringly and I so want to believe him. I want to hear his words and clutch them to my heart and keep them there in a gilded cage.

But then he speaks again. "You're not safe, Calla. You have to come with me now. There's something you need to know."

I'm frozen, petrified by my circumstances. Go with him to Whitley? With a person I don't even know anymore, *with a person I think I should be afraid of?* Confusion consumes me and nothing seems real.

Nothing but two things.

I have to admit that I *do* feel the danger. It crackles around me, everywhere. It's here for me. I just don't know why.

You're not safe, Calla.

And of course, Dare. He's here, he's real, and I love him.

But.

I can't trust him.

I can't trust anything.

"I don't know what to do," I whisper jaggedly. "I want to hate you, Dare, for lying to me. But I can't." I'm too confused, and he's my anchor.

He grabs my arm and pulls me to him, resisting my struggles, and then I'm limp.

Because here, surrounded by his scent and his warmth and his strength… this is where I belong. How can I argue with that?

"You belong right here, with me," he tells me, his lips moving against my hair. *"You don't hate me, Calla.* You can't. I didn't lie to you. I tried to tell you."

His voice is afraid, terrified actually, and it touches a soft place in me, a hidden place, the place where I protect my love for him. The place where my heart used to be before it was so broken.

"You're my own personal anti-Christ," I whisper into his shirt. His hands stroke my hair frantically, trailing down my back and clutching me to him. "Why can't you just tell me everything right now?"

"Because I can't," he rasps. "Because things are complicated, and unless you uncover it yourself, you'll think I'm a monster. I love you, Calla. I *will* protect you. You just have to trust me."

I yank back now, grasping at my courage and my strength. *"Trust you?* You must be joking."

He's surprised, and I'm shattered as I sprint down the beach, my feet sinking in the wet sand, the wind whipping my hair.

I love Dare, more than anything, but I can't trust him. The only person I've ever been able to truly trust is dead.

I need my brother.

I need Finn.

I race up the trail, into my house, and up to my brother's room.

It's exactly like he left it.

I sink to my heels just inside the door.

The walls close in on me, four of them and the ceiling, coming closer, swallowing me, crushing me. I cover my ears and rock back and forth because amid everything, I still hear my brother's voice.

It'll be ok. It'll be ok. It'll be ok.

I can't keep hearing voices.

Not even Finn's.

I can't.

I can't.

I'm sane, Goddamnit.

I'm overwhelmed by Dare's lies, by my fear... and by the very real fact that I'm so very fragile.

"Her hold on reality is tenuous."

It's a murmur that cuts through my panic.

I pause, halting all movement, not even breathing. The whisper comes from the other side of the door.

"No, I don't want to do that. Not yet." The voice, hissing and firm, and it can't be real. There's no way. I'm frozen as it envelopes me, as reality slithers further away.

"We have to. She wouldn't want this."

Confused, I stare at the wooden planes of the door, at the grain.

Is this really happening?

Or is my mind playing tricks on me yet again?

I gulp and draw in a shaky breath.

"Anything could send her back over the edge," the familiar voice cautions, his voice careful and low and familiar. There's no way it can be him. There's no way.

Even still, I want to wrap myself in the sound, to hide in it, to escape in it.

But I can't.

Because the answer is immediate.

"That's why we have to handle her carefully."

Handle me?

The door opens and I look up to find three shadows looming over me.

My father.

Dare.

And someone I can't see, a faceless, nameless figure lurking in the shadows. I peer closely, trying to see if it's him, even while knowing in my heart that it can't be Finn.

It's impossible.

I scoot backward until my spine is against my brother's bed. I'm a skittish fawn, and they're my hunters. I'm prey because I'm in danger, and I don't know why.

But they do.

"Calla," my dad says, kindly and soothingly. "You're ok. *You're ok.* But I need you to trust me right now."

His face is grave and pale. I look at Dare and notice that his hands are clenched into fists, his knuckles white. The air in this room is charged now, dangerous, and I find that I can scarcely breathe.

I brace myself.

Because deep in the pit of my stomach I feel like I can't trust anyone.

I squeeze my eyes shut, and push my face into Finn's blanket. Through the muffled fabric, I hear words. I feel Dare's hand on my shoulder. I feel the vibration of his deep voice in my chest.

And then I feel his absence.

I open my eyes.

The room is empty.

They'd given up.

Whatever they wanted to tell me, I'm safe from it now.

Because I'm alone.

With shaky steps, I climb to my feet and walk to Finn's nightstand. I pick up his St. Michael's medallion and fasten it around my neck.

Holding it in my fingers, I whisper the prayer, each word quick and stiff on my lips.

St. Michael the Archangel, defend us in battle. Be our defense against the wickedness and snares of the Devil. May God rebuke him, we humbly pray, and do thou, O Prince of the heavenly hosts, by the power of God, thrust into hell Satan, and all the evil spirits, who prowl about the world seeking the ruin of souls. Amen.

I say the prayer three times in a row, just to make sure.

I'm protected.

I'm protected.

I'm protected.

I'm safe now. I'm wearing Finn's medallion. I'm safe.

I'm just drawing a shaky breath of relief when the door creaks open again and I'm faced once again with my insanity.

My startled eyes flash upward, finding the impossible.

Finn.

My dead brother.

VERUM

Standing in the doorway of his bedroom.

Chapter Two

"You're ok," Finn tells me quickly, his gaze connected with mine, and with lips that are supposed to be dead. He sees my panic, he sees my terror. Because he knows me best.

Quickly, he crosses the room and kneels beside me, his hands cold as he grabs mine and holds them.

St. Michael the Archangel, defend us in battle.

It can't be him. But yet, as I stare down at Finn's white fingers, and the pale freckle that splotches across his middle knuckle, I know it's him. It has to be. I know that freckle, I know those hands.

"Finn," I manage to say, a whisper.

He nods. And he's warm. Confused, I slide my hand against his chest, finding what I need to know. A heart beats against my hand, strong and true through this thin ribcage.

Ba-bump.

Ba-bump.

Ba-bump.

No.

This can't be.

"It is," he nods again, and I realize that I'd spoken aloud.

Be our defense against the wickedness and snares of the Devil.

"Am I insane?" I ask limply, and all feelings have fled my body. I'm numb. I'm a piece of wood. I'm a sponge, and I have no feelings, and I've absorbed all of this insanity for so long that now I'm insane myself. That's the only possible answer.

Finn's slender arm stretches behind me, curling around my shoulder, and I'm limp against his chest, my ear pressed to his heart to make absolute sure.

Ba-bump.

Ba-bump.

Ba-bump.

"This is impossible."

My words are whispers. Three of them. Six syllables of impossibility.

"You can't trust your own mind right now, Cal," he tells me solemnly, his pale blue eyes so light and clean and familiar. "So you're going to have to trust me instead."

I do. He's the only one.

He knows that.

But...

Reality isn't this. Reality is a red smashed car and a white tombstone. *Good night, sweet Finn.*

There were dragonflies and sunlight that day. There was a cemetery and tears.

25

May God rebuke him, we humbly pray, and do thou, O Prince of the heavenly hosts, by the power of God, thrust into hell Satan.

"How can this be?" I ask tremulously, afraid to trust it, afraid to hope.

Finn looks away, his hands still wrapped around mine.

And all the evil spirits, who prowl about the world seeking the ruin of souls. Amen.

"Because it just is," he says firmly. "I can't tell you. You have to come to it. But you will, Cal. You will."

Oh God, we're back to that. We're back to the "I can't tell you because it will annihilate you" thing.

My chest deflates.

My breath rushes out.

I can't do this again.

Not this.

It's too much.

Finn sees my expression and catches me when I fall against him, limp and discouraged. *He always catches me.*

"Your mind is an amazing thing," he assures me. "It's a gift, not a curse."

He knows me so well. He knew what I'd been thinking.

"Are you real?" I ask in a whisper, as my eyes shutter closed.

He smiles.

That's the last thing I see.

Then it's blissfully, blessedly black.

Thank you, St. Michael.

When I wake, it's dark. The room is shadowy, but I realize very quickly that I'm no longer in Finn's room. I'm in a different bed, in my pajamas, with clean sheets wrapped around my hand.

I stare at the ceiling, at the walls, at the shadows, and then I stare at the figure sitting beside my bed, hidden in the dark.

"Finn?" I ask quietly, expecting it to be my brother.

I don't expect the voice that answers.

"Calla-Lily."

Dare.

Of course. Finn can't be here, because Finn is dead.

I swallow as Dare leans forward, as the square of his jaw falls into the moonlight, as his eyes glint.

"Are you real?"

I whisper.

He smiles his *Dare Me* grin.

"I'm here, aren't I?" he answers quietly.

"That doesn't mean anything these days." My voice is small. "I can't take much more, Dare. I don't understand anything."

"I've failed you," Dare gets up from his seat and kneels next to me, his face earnest and dark and tortured. "I've failed you. But I'll fix it."

"How?" I whisper, and I don't think I want to know. "How have you failed me? What have you done?"

I can't.

I can't know.

I can't know or it might kill me.

My mind is a hollow reed and the breeze is blowing through it, blowing all of the pieces away. I want to chase them, but I can't.

My hand is anchored by Dare's.

His fingers shake, and I suddenly know what I have to do.

I have to step away from the man I love.

I have to

I have to

I have to.

Because I can't take it otherwise.

My mind is elastic, and it's going to snap.

"I've done a terrible thing," he confesses, and each word is staccato. "I don't expect your forgiveness. But I have to fix it. And to do that, I need your help. You have to help me, Calla. Help me save you."

Save me, and I'll save you.

Right?

I feel... I feel... I feel.

I feel a wave of déjà vu. I feel a wave of emotion, of sensation, of things I should know but don't.

"What have you done?" I ask him through fractured thoughts. "What do I need saving from? From you? Because I don't think I can be saved."

"You're wrong," he insists, and his eyes beg me. "I can save you."

I shake my head and the movement is painful. "There's only one way," I whisper and the words hurt my soul. "You have to leave me alone, Dare. You have to let me go. I can't take anymore. I can't take the secrets."

"You love me," he reminds me, his stare cutting me into pieces.

"I know," I whisper, throwing those pieces away. "But I don't think that's enough right now. I'm going to break, Dare. I'm going to break."

I draw my knees to my chest and look away, taking a deep shaky breath.

"I know I sound crazy," I admit. "I know it. But I can't help what I feel. I have to protect myself from you. I know that much is true. My heart is telling me to be afraid of you."

And it is. It's telling me there's a reason.

I feel it in my bones, in my hollow reed bones.

Dare closes his eyes, and it is minutes before he opens them, and when he does, they're so empty, so lost.

"Fine," he says simply. "Protect yourself from me. Hell, *I'll* protect you from me. But come with me to Whitley. That's where you'll find the answers. You can have your space, you'll have peace and quiet, and you'll recover, Cal."

"The answers are at Whitley?"

I stare at Dare, at the body I love, the eyes that I can fall into, the heart that has held me up... and hidden so many secrets.

He nods, and it's like the movement is painful for him. He doesn't want to go to Whitley, but he's willing to go for me.

"Your dad wants you to go," he adds. "Can you do it for him?"

Can I?

An overpowering sense of foreboding cripples me, almost sending me to my knees. I don't know. I only know... if I don't find answers, I might lose my sanity.

The answers are at Whitley.

I exhale, realizing that I'd been holding my breath. "Ok. I'll go."

For answers, and for my father. Because he's been through enough already. He shouldn't have to watch me fall apart.

Dare's beautiful eyes shutter closed. "I love you, Calla."

Pain ripples through me to the point of being physical, to the point of stopping my aching heart.

"I know."

But I don't think that's enough.

I don't say it.

Because he already knows. I see it on his tortured face.

I ache to reach out and touch it, to sooth him, to hold him.

But I can't.

There's something to fear here.

And until I know what it is, I have to distance myself.

It's the only way I'll survive.

Chapter Three

The plane ride is long, even though we're in first class.

A flight attendant pays personal attention to me, bringing me blankets and warm cloths and icy drinks, and the whole flight, I'm on pins and needles with Dare.

Because I love him.

Because he's a stranger to me now.

Seated next to me, in the wide leather seat, he tries to engage me in conversation, tries to pull me out of my shell, but I avoid every effort.

It's so painfully, impossibly hard, but I have to.

I have to until I know what he's hiding.

He's hurt, I can tell. Because my actions are painful. They're painful to us both. But there's something giant and black and scary hanging over my head, and I can't let it fall on us.

Everything depends on me. I know that much is true.

But what is *everything?* I don't know.

The perfectly made-up flight attendant bends next to me. "Only a few minutes until our descent into Heathrow. Is there anything you need?"

My sanity, please.

I shake my head and she's gone, and before long, we're walking into the busy airport. Dare's hand is on my elbow, and even though I don't want to, I shake it away.

His mouth is tight and he leans into my ear.

"You're not safe, Calla. Whether you like it or not, you have to stay with me right now."

I'm dumbfounded and he takes my elbow and I let him.

I'm not safe.

I'm in a fog as we walk to a tall man in a black chauffeur's uniform waiting on the edge of the corridor. He's got gray hair and a bulbous nose, and his face is thin and stern, but I see a flicker of warmth when he sees me. He looks at Dare, though, and his face cools.

"Mr. DuBray," he nods as we approach, and for a second, I think he has mistaken us for someone else. But Dare answers.

"I hope the car is nearby, Jones. We're exhausted."

The man's mouth presses firmly together. "It's right outside, sir." And somehow, I feel like he resents Dare. But he still takes our bags and we follow him outside to where a sleek black limousine waits. It's long and glitzy and I've never been in a limousine before. My eyes widen.

What kind of family am I from?

To date, I've been solidly middle-class with a mortician for a father. We live in a funeral home and Finn and I have been the butt of a million jokes in school. We've been surrounded by death, isolated on the top of a mountain, *freaks.*

But here... *here...* I think it might be different.

Maybe.

"You must be Calla," Jones observes as he takes my bag. I nod.

"Yes."

"You look just like your mother," he tells me, and there is warmth for a second in his eyes, and I swallow hard because I miss her, because I'd do anything if she could just be here with me right now. "Welcome to England."

"Thank you," I murmur as he opens my door, then loads our suitcases into the trunk.

As the car pulls away from the curb, I close my eyes and press my forehead to the window, trying to force it all to fade away.

I'm not alone.

I didn't lose my mother and brother.

I don't have to give up the man I love.

I try hard to will it away.

But I know from experience it won't work, from the million times I've tried it in school, to try and hide myself from sneers and taunts.

It never worked then, and it doesn't work now.

I'm still here in England, I'm still alone, I'm not safe from *something*, although I don't know from what. The man I love is next to me, but he might as well be a million miles away... because I can't trust him anymore. Because my mind is fragile, and even I know it.

So since I can't make it all fade away, I focus on the good points.

I'm going somewhere quiet, somewhere away from the sadness. I'll be able to focus, to repair myself, to get answers.

I'm driving away from the airport in luxury. I pause at this.

If Finn were here, he'd be agog at the glitz of this car, at the fancy bottled water sitting in ice just for us, or the rolled up towels in a little steamer. We've never been pampered like this before, and with a lump in my throat, I decide it's not fair that Finn isn't here.

Because he'll never be pampered like this now.

If Finn can't use this stuff, then I won't either.

I resist the water and the towels, and the tiny chocolate mints. I won't have any of it.

I open my eyes, watching out the window as the bustle of the city turns into the quiet of the country.

"Take the scenic route, Jones," Dare calls up to the driver. Jones doesn't answer, but he does deviate from his route, and before long, I see glimpses of the ocean here and there among the trees and rocks.

"We live a little ways from Hastings. It's close to Sussex," Dare tells me, as though I know anything at all about English geography. I nod like I do, because so much of what we say is a pretense now. We go through the motions.

Thirty minutes later, our car is still gliding over the winding ribbons of road, but I finally see a rooftop in the distance, spires and towers poking through trees.

Dare stirs, opening his eyes, and I know we're almost there.

I crane my neck to see. When I do, I'm stunned beyond words, enough that the breath hitches on my lips.

This can't be my family's home.

It's huge, it's lavish, it's creepy.

It's ancient, it's stone, it's beautiful.

A tall stone wall stretches in either direction as far as I can see, encircling the property like an ominous security blanket. It's so tall, so heavy, and for one brief moment, I wonder if it's meant to keep people out... or to keep them in.

It's a foolish notion, I know.

As we pull off the road, large wrought iron gates open in front of our car as if by magic, as if they were pushed by unseen hands. Puffs of mist and fog swirl from the ground and through the tree branches, half concealing whatever lies behind the gate.

Even though the grounds are lush and green, there's something heavy here, something dark. It's more than the near constant rain, more than the clouds.

Something that I can't quite put my finger on.

I'm filled with a strange dread as the car rolls through the gates, as we continue toward the hidden thing. And while the 'hidden thing' is just a house, it feels like so much more, like something ominous and almost threatening.

I catch glimpses of it through the branches as we drive, and each glimpse gives me pause.

A steep, gabled roof.

Columns and spires and moss.

Rain drips from the trees, onto the car, onto the driveway, and everything gleams with a muted light.

It's wet here, and gray, and the word I keep thinking in my head is *gothic.*

Gothic.

Despite all the beauty and the extravagance here, it still looks a bit terrifying.

I count the beats as we make our way to the house, and I've counted to fifteen before the limousine finally comes to a stop on top of a giant circular driveway made of cobblestone.

The house in front of us is made from stone, and it sprawls out as far as I can see. The windows are dark, in all sizes, in all shapes.

Rolling, manicured lawns, an enormous mansion, lush gardens. Stormy clouds roll behind the massive setting of the house, and one thing is clear. Ominous or not, this estate is lavish, to say the least.

"Is my family rich?" I ask dumbly.

Dare glances at me. "Not in the ways that matter."

He pauses, and there is a rope between us, pulling us together, but at the same time, coiling around us, holding us apart.

"Calla, don't let your guard down," he tells me quickly. "This place... it isn't what it seems. You have to..."

Jones opens the door, and Dare stops speaking abruptly.

I have to what?

"Welcome to Whitley," Jones tells me with a slight bow. Dare and I climb out and suddenly, I'm nervous.

I'm in a foreign country, getting ready to meet a family consisting of strangers, and I know nothing about them.

It's daunting.

Dare squeezes my hand briefly, and I let him. Because here, I'm alone.

Here, Dare is the only familiar thing.

Here, he's the only one who knows me.

Jones leads the way with our bags, and before we even reach the front doors, they open, and a small wrinkled woman stands in the doorway. She's slightly bent, barely a wisp of a woman, with an olive complexion and her hair completely wrapped in a brightly covered scarf twisted at the top. She looks like she might be a hundred years old.

"Sabine!" Dare greets the elderly woman in a warm hug. The little woman's arm close around him, and her head barely reaches his chest.

"Welcome home, boy," she says in a deep gravely voice. "I've missed you."

Dare pulls away and glances at me, and I can see on his face that Sabine is important. At least to him. "This is Sabine. She was my nanny growing up. And your mother's nanny, too. Sabine, this is Calla Price."

Sabine stares at me, curiously, sadly.

"You're the spitting image of your mother," she tells me.

"I know," I tell her, and my heart twinges because my mother is gone. "It's nice to meet you."

I offer her my hand, but she grasps it instead of shaking it. Stooping over, she examines it, her face mere inches from my palm. She grips me tight, unwilling to let me go, and I feel my pulse bounding wildly against her fingers.

Startled, I wait.

I don't know what else to do.

The little woman is surprisingly strong, her grip holding me steady as she searches for something in my hand. She traces the veins and the ridges, her breath hot on my skin. Her face is so close to my palm that I can feel each time she exhales.

If Finn were here, he'd be laughing so hard right now.

But he's not, and so there's no one to share this hilarity with, because even though he wishes it weren't true, Dare fits in here. He's one of them and I'm not.

Abruptly, Sabine drops my hand and straightens.

Her eyes meet mine and I see a thousand lifetimes in hers. They're dark as obsidian, and unlike most elderly people, hers aren't cloudy with age. She stares into me, and I feel like she's literally sifting through my thoughts and looking into my soul.

It's unsettling, and a chill runs up my spine, putting me on edge.

She glances at Dare, and nods ever so slightly.

If I didn't know better, I would almost think he cringed.

What the hell?

But I don't have time to ponder, because Sabine starts walking, leading us into the house.

"Come. Eleanor is waiting for you," Sabine tells us solemnly over her shoulder as she uses much of her strength to open the heavy front doors.

Dare sighs. "I think we'd better freshen up first. It's been a long flight, Sabby."

The nanny looks sympathetic, but is unrelenting. "I'm sorry, Dare. She insists on seeing you both."

Dare sighs again, but we obediently follow Sabine through lavish hallways. Over marble floors and lush rugs, through mahogany paneled halls and extravagant window dressings, beneath sparkling crystal chandeliers. My eyes are wide as we take it all in. I've never seen such a house in all my life, not even on TV.

But even as it is opulent, it's silent.

It's still.

It's like living in a mausoleum.

We come to a stop in front of massive wooden doors, ornately carved. Sabine knocks on them twice, and a woman's voice calls out from within.

"Enter."

How eerily formal.

Sabine opens the doors, and we are immediately enveloped by an overwhelmingly large study, painted in rich colors and patinas, encircled with wooden shelves filled by hundreds and hundreds of leather-bound books.

A woman sits at the heavy cherry desk, facing us with her back to the windows.

Her face is stern, her hair is faded, but I can see that it used to be red. It's pulled into a severe chignon, not one strand out of place. Her cashmere sweater is buttoned all the way to the top, decorated by one single strand of pearls. Her unadorned hands are folded in front of her and she's waiting.

Waiting for us.

How long has she been waiting? Months? Years?

For a reason that I can't explain, I feel suffocated. The room seems to close in on me, and I'm frozen. Dare has to literally pull me, then pull me harder, just to make me move.

I feel like I can't breathe, like if I approach her, something bad will happen.

Something terrible.

It's a ridiculous thought, and Dare glances at me out of the corner of his eye.

We come to a stop in front of the desk.

"Eleanor," he says tightly.

There is no love lost here. I can see it. I can sense it. I feel it in the air, in the formality, in the cold.

"Adair," the woman nods. There are no hugs, no smiles. Even though it's been at least a year since she's seen him, this woman doesn't even stand up.

"This is your grandmother, Eleanor Savage," Dare tells me, and his words are so carefully calm. Eleanor stares at me, her gaze examining me from head to toe. My cheeks flush from it.

"You must be Calla."

I nod.

"You may call me Eleanor." She glances at the door. "Wait outside, Sabine."

Without a word, Sabine backs out, closing the door. Eleanor returns her attention to us.

"I'm sorry for your loss," she tells me stiffly, but her voice lacks any sign of emotion, of sympathy or sadness, even though it was her daughter who was lost. She didn't know Finn, so I can understand that, but her own daughter?

She looks at me again. "While you are here, Whitley will be your home. You will not intrude in rooms that don't concern you. You may have the run of the grounds, you may use the stables. You won't mingle with unsavory characters, you may have use of the car. Jones will drive you wherever you need to go. You may settle in, get accustomed to life in the country, and soon, we'll speak about your inheritance. Since you've turned eighteen, you have responsibilities to this family."

She pauses, then looks at me.

"You've suffered a loss, but life goes on. You will learn to go on, as well."

She looks away from us, directing her attention to a paper on her desk. "Sabine!" she calls, without looking up.

Apparently, we've been dismissed.

Sabine re-enters and Dare and I quickly follow her, jumping at the chance to leave this distasteful woman.

"Well, she's pleasant," I mutter.

Dare's lip tilts.

"She's not my favorite."

Understatement.

We share a moment, a warm moment, but I shove it away.

43

I can't.

I can't.

Sabine stops in front of double wooden doors.

"This was your mother's suite," Sabine tells me. "It's yours now. Dare's room is across the house." After she says that, she waits, as if she's expecting a reaction from me. When she doesn't get one, she continues. "Dinner will be at seven in the dining room. Be prompt. You should rest now."

She turns and walks away, shuffling down the hall on tiny feet.

Dare stares at me, tall and slender. "Do you want me to stay with you?"

"No." My answer is immediate and harsh.

He's startled and he pulls away a bit, staring down at me.

"I just... I need to be alone," I add.

I'm not strong enough to resist you yet.

Disappointment gleams in his eyes, but to his credit, he doesn't press me. He swallows his hurt and nods.

"Ok. I'm wiped out, so I'm going to take a nap before dinner. I suggest you do the same. You must be tired."

I nod because he's right, I'm utterly exhausted. He's gone, and I'm left alone in the long quiet hallway.

I take a step toward my bedroom, then another, but for the life of me, I can't seem to turn the doorknob.   Something settles around me, dread, I think, and I just can't do it.

The look on Eleanor's face emerges in my head, the way she was examining me, and I can't breathe. Something crushes me, that dark thing that I felt in the driveway.   It feels like it's here, pushing on me, lapping at me.

I know it doesn't make any sense.

Something pulls me.

It pulls me right into my mother's old rooms.

And there, I sit, surrounded by her memories.

Chapter Four

My mother's rooms are as lavish as the rest of the house. There are no childhood posters taped to the walls here, no teenage heart-throbs, no pink phones or plush pillows.

The suite is carefully decorated, with heavy off-white furniture and sage green walls. The bed is massive, covered in thick blankets, all sage green, all soothing.

But it's not the room of a child, or a teenager, or even a young woman.

It lacks youthful energy.

But I still feel her here.

Somehow.

Sinking onto the bed, I find that I'm surrounded by windows.

All along one wall, they stretch from floor to ceiling. They let in the dying evening light, and I feel exposed. Getting to my feet, I pull the drapes closed.

I feel a little safer now, but not much.

My suitcases are stacked inside the door, and so I set about unpacking. I put my sweaters away, my toiletries in the fancy bathroom, and while I'm standing on the marble tiles, I envision my mother here.

She loved a good bath, and this bathtub is fit for a queen.

I imagine her soaking here, reading a good book, and my eyes well up.

She's gone.

I know that.

I pull open the closet doors, and for a moment, a very brief moment, I swear I catch a whiff of her perfume.

She's worn the same scent for as long as I've known her.

There are shelves in this walk-in closet, and on one, I see a bottle of Chanel.

Her scent.

I clutch it to me, and inhale it, and it brings a firestorm of memories down on my head. Of my mother laughing, of her baking cookies, of her grinning at me over the top of her book.

With burning eyes, I put the bottle back.

This isn't helping anything.

I hang my shirts and my sweaters.

There's a knock on the door, and Sabine comes in with a tray. A teapot and a cup.

"I brought you some tea," she tells me quietly, setting it on a table. "It'll perk you up. Traveling is hard on a person."

Losing their entire life is hard on a person.

But of course I don't say that.

I just smile and say thank you.

She pours me a cup and hands it to me.

"This will help you rest. It's calming."

I sip at it, and Sabine turns around, surveying my empty bags.

"I see you've already unpacked. These rooms haven't been changed since your mother left."

I hold my cup in my lap, warming my fingers because the chill from the English evening has left them cold.

"Why *did* my mother leave?" I ask, because she's never said. She's never said *anything* about her childhood home.

Sabine pauses, and when she looks at me, she's looking into my soul again, rooting around with wrinkled fingers.

"She left because she had to," Sabine says simply. "Whitley couldn't hold her."

It's an answer that's not an answer.

I should've expected no less.

Sabine sits next to me, patting my leg.

"I'll fatten you up a bit here," she tells me. "You're too skinny, like your mama. You'll rest and you'll… see things for what they are."

"And how is that?" I ask tiredly, and suddenly I'm so very exhausted.

Sabine looks at my face and clucks.

"Child, you need to rest. You're fading away in front of my eyes. Come now. Lie down."

She settles me onto the bed, pulling a blanket up to my chin.

"Dinner is at seven," she reminds me before she leaves. "Sleep until then."

I try.

I really do.

I close my eyes.

I relax my arms and my legs and my muscles.

But sleep won't come.

Eventually, I give up, and I open the drapes and look outside.

The evening is quiet, the sky is dark. *It gets dark so early here.*

The trees rustle in the breeze, and the wind is wet. It's cold. It's chilling. I can feel it even through the windows and I rub at my arms.

That's when I get goose-bumps.

They lift the hair on my neck,

And the stars seem to mock me.

Turning my back on them, I cross the room and pull a book from a shelf.

Jane Eyre.

Fitting, given Whitley and the moors and the rain.

I open the cover and find a penned inscription.

To Laura. May you always have the spirit of Charlotte Bronte and the courage to follow your dreams. Your father.

The ink is fading, and I run my fingertips across it.

The message lacks tenderness, but it's still telling.

My grandfather supported my mother wanting to be independent. Somehow, I doubt Eleanor shared that same sentiment.

I slip into a seat with it, pulling open the pages, my eyes trying to devour the words my mother once read.

But I've only gotten to the part where Jane proclaims that she hates long walks on cold afternoons when I hear something.

I feel something.

I feel a growl in my bones.

It's low and threatening, and it vibrates my ribs.

I startle upright, looking around, but of course, I'm still alone.

But the growl happens again, low and long.

My breath hitches and the book hits the floor, the pages fluttering on the rug.

A sudden panic overtakes me, rapid and hot.

I have to get out.

I don't know why.

It's a feeling I have in my heart, something that drives me from my mother's rooms out into the hall, because something is chasing me.

I feel it on my heels.

I feel it breathing down my neck.

Without looking back, I rush back down the corridor, through the house and out the front doors.

I've got to breathe.

I've got to breathe.

I've got to breathe.

Sucking in air, I walk aimlessly around the house, over the cobblestone and down a pathway. I draw in long even breaths, trying to still my shaking hands, trying to gather myself together, trying to assure myself that I'm being silly.

There's no reason to be afraid.

I'm being ridiculous.

This house might be strange and foreign, but it's still a home. It just isn't *my* home. It's fine. I'll get used to it.

I look behind me, and there's nothing there.

There is no growl, there is no vibration in my ribs, there is nothing but for the dim twilight and the stars aching to burst from behind the clouds.

The house looms over me and I circle back, only to find myself in front of a large garage with gabled edges.

There are at least seven garage doors, all closed but one.

To my surprise, someone walks out of that door.

A boy.

A man.

His pants are dark gray and he's wearing a hoodie, and he moves with grace. He slides among the shadows with ease, as though he belongs here, as though Whitley is his home too, even though I don't know him.

"Hello," I call out to him.

He stops moving, freezing in his tracks, but he doesn't turn his head.

Something about that puts me on edge and I tense, because what if he's not supposed to be here?

"Hello?" I repeat uneasily, and chills run up my spine, goose-bumps forming on my arms once again.

I back away, first one step, then another.

I blink,

And he's gone.

I stare at the empty space, and shake my head, blinking hard.

He's still gone.

He must've slipped between the buildings, but why?

I hurry back to my room, too nervous to find out.

I'm still unsettled as I wash my face, so when I'm finished, I poke my head out into the hall. There's nothing there.

With a sigh, I lock my bedroom door and I'm chilled from the wet English air. Glancing at the clock, I find it's only six thirty. I can rest for a few minutes more, and I'm thankful for that.

Because clearly, jet lag has made me its bitch.

I close my eyes.

It all whirls around.

I stand in the clouds and spread my arms and spinandspinandspin.

No one can touch me here.

It's not real here, but it is there.

Down there, it's cold and wet.

It's uncomfortable there, silent and awkward and rigid.

The eyes are the worst, each of them turned toward me... watching me, waiting for something. For what?

My skin crawls and I scratch it til it bleeds because I'd rather not have it than let it crawl away.

They can't get to me.

I won't let them.

I don't know them.

And I don't want to.

Chapter Five

Dinner at Whitley is a formal, uncomfortable affair.

I feel horribly underdressed as Eleanor sits at the head of the table in a tailored skirt suit and the same strand of pearls. I'm fidgety, a tell-tale sign that I feel out of place. If anyone knew me here, they'd know.

"Tell me of your schooling," Eleanor directs from far down the table. The gleaming table is so long, I feel the need to shout whenever I speak.

I'm in the middle of explaining public school to her when the doors open at nine minutes past the hour. Eleanor watches in stern disapproval as Dare enters the quiet room.

Thank you, God, I exhale. It's like I hold my breath when Dare isn't with me, and it's a habit I need to change.

Tall and elegant, he slides into a place next to me, dressed in slacks and a suit jacket, a cobalt shirt open at the collar. He looks just as at home in the suit as he does in jeans, and a bit of his dark hair drifts down over his eye. He tosses it back as he sits.

Every tiny piece of my being is relieved that he's here, and I try to ignore the feeling.

He's not my security blanket, not anymore.

He can't be.

"How nice of you to join us," Eleanor says stiffly, before returning her attention back to me. It's as though she doesn't want to be bothered by him, as though he's an intrusion. But he clearly belongs here all the same.

I can't help but steal another glance at him and when I do, I find him staring at me.

He doesn't look away, and his eyes are a smoldering midnight sky.

I swallow hard, and Eleanor notices.

She clears her throat.

"Adair, that isn't your chair. You know your place is across the table."

Astonished, I stare at her. There must be twenty places at this table and only three of them are taken. Surely it doesn't matter where he sits.

"I'll be sitting here tonight," his answer is cool. My relief is immeasurable.

Eleanor doesn't push it.

"Regardless of where you sit, dinner is at seven. *Promptly* at seven. You know that. If you're late, don't bother attending."

Dare doesn't seem concerned. He stares back at her.

"Noted."

His voice is deep and husky and cold.

For the rest of dinner, the only noise in the room is silver scraping against china.

It's uncomfortable, and it's silent.

If only Finn were here.

He'd be kicking me beneath the table, rolling his eyes, making me laugh.

But he's not.

I'm alone.

And I've never felt so uneasy.

Except for when I encountered the strange man earlier.

"Is there someone else living here?" I ask suddenly, and Eleanor looks up from her fruit.

"Pardon me?" she raises her eyebrow.

"Earlier," I explain. "I was restless so I went for a walk outside. There was a guy out there in a hoodie. He seemed out of place."

Dare and Eleanor exchange a glance.

"What did he look like?" Dare asks me quietly, his eyes frozen on mine.

I shrug. "I couldn't see his face, he had his hood up. He was young, though. Sort of skinny."

Silence.

Finally, Dare clears his throat. "There's no one else here, Calla. Aside from Jones and Sabine, we have a groomsman for the stable, but he's an elderly man. There is a gardening team, but they come here early in the morning before anyone is out of bed."

"Then who was it?" I ask, confused, and a bit afraid.

Dare stares at me. "Maybe you just *thought* you saw someone."

I flush, because of my recent history, it's no wonder they don't believe me. The heat spreads to my chest, and I fight the urge to fan myself.

"I… maybe," I finally agree.

I'm jet-lagged. I'm tired. I'm overwhelmed. It's quite possible that I hadn't seen him at all. Because I'd also thought my room was growling.

"I hate this place," I mutter to myself when we're finally released. Dare overhears me and increases his long strides so he catches up to me.

"It's not that bad," he tells me. "It's what you make of it, as long as you never let your guard down."

I glance at him, and *God, I miss him.*

We pass in front of a window and the moonlight bathes his face, and I want to touch his lips with my fingers.

He walks me to my room.

"Tell me more about the guy you saw outside," he says softly, and his fingers find mine. They wrap around my hand, warm and familiar, and I want to close my eyes.

"No," I finally answer. "You're right. My eyes were probably playing tricks on me. I was really tired."

Dare's gaze is doubtful. Concerned.

"Do you want me to stay with you?" he asks, and his tone is hopeful.

Everything in me screams to say yes, to let him hold me until I sleep, to soak up his familiarity and warmth, but I shake my head because my heart is still afraid.

And there must be a reason why.

"That's ok. You don't need to babysit me. I'm ok, Dare. I promise."

It's a lie.

I'm not.

But he can't make it better.

He cocks his head.

"Dare, I... I need some space."

"Some space?"

I nod. "Yeah. I need to come to grips with things, to wrap my head around... Finn, and you, and I ... I need space."

There's silence, and the air is charged and I ache to fold into him, to let him hold all of my fears at bay, but I can't. I can't be weak. Something big, bigger than me, depends on it. I just don't know what yet.

He finally nods. "Ok. I'll give you some space. If you need me, text me and I'll be here in two minutes."

I nod and he bends, pressing his lips to my forehead. I don't shirk away.

After he leaves me, I enter my lonely bedroom and sit on my lonely bed and inhale the lonely air.

"I miss you, Finn," I breathe aloud. Because he always 'got me', no matter what. I never had to explain, I never had to elaborate. Things could go unspoken.

It was a twin thing.

But now he's gone and I'm alone.

It's not a comfortable place, to be a half without a whole.

I glance around my room. It's large and expansive and the chair in front of the windows beckons me, and I slouch into it, pulling my knees to my chest, picking back up *Jane Eyre.*

Below me, outside, the English moors roll on for miles, yawning across the perimeter of Whitley. Whitley is so similar to Thornfield Hall that Charlotte Bronte could've written her book from my windows.

As I watch, fog rises up from the ground, shrouding everything in mist.

It's just when I'm glancing away to read my book that I see the movement.

I fixate again on the moors.

Focusing harder, I wait for it, almost expecting to see the mysterious man from earlier.

But it's Dare.

He walks along the path from the gardens, gliding along in the night, his stride wide and familiar.

Then he stops.

He must feel me staring at him because he looks up.

He turns his dark head and his gaze finds me.

It's as though he can see me watching, all the way from the stable.

His eyes are blacker than night, and he has found me.

His gaze is hot and I close my eyes, my breathing shallow.

When I open them, he's gone.

But the strange feeling, the odd thought, lingers with me.

He's dangerous.

I'm unsafe.

And he has found me.

What a strange thought.

But then again, I'm a strange girl.

***

Breakfast and lunch are just as formal and uncomfortable at Whitley as dinner is.

After a morning of sitting uncomfortably alone, I manage to slip away without Sabine noticing. She's been watching me, and I fear that she's waiting for her chance to pin me down, to talk to me more about my mother.

I can't do that.

Not yet.

As I burst into the fresh air of the outdoors, I tilt my face to the sun and draw in a deep breath.

God, it feels good to be free.

Startled, I realize that even though I'm nervous of this place, it's still a welcome break from my reality back home.

The suffocating daily life of a girl who lives in a funeral home.

Back home, everyone knows what I am. A sad girl who lost most of her family and went crazy. I'll never shake those things off, I'll never just be normal.

But I'm free of it here.

For now.

Until I'm here long enough and they figure it all out.

Sighing, I head down the cobbled path toward the stables, intent on exploring the property, on seeing everything there is to see.

My feet crunch on the stone, my lungs expanding as I breathe.

I'm startled when a shadow steps out from the building.

My gasp is louder than I intend, and Dare looks up.

He's dressed in dark jeans and a black shirt. The pieces fit him so well, they look tailored specifically for him. It seems that no matter what he wears, he's perfectly at home in the clothing.

He arcs an eyebrow as he pauses on the path.

"Are you lost?"

His tone is careful, almost abrupt. He's giving me space, trying not to crowd me, just like I requested. He's hesitant to open himself to me now, because I've already rejected him.

It feels odd, like he's a stranger, and I don't like it but I don't stop it.

Because it has to be.

It has to be *for now.*

I shuffle my feet nervously.

"No. I'm just looking around."

"Would you like company?" he asks, and he's poised to join me.

It would be so easy, to just say yes.

But...something is in his eyes.

Something that I've seen before, but I can't remember.

The fear swells back up in my stomach and I shake my head.

"No, thank you," I answer finally, and Dare's dark eyes close. He's guarded now so I can't hurt him. "I think I'll just explore on my own. I don't want to waste your time."

"You've never been a waste of my time," he tells me, and his tone is oddly formal.

He walks on, past me, and for a minute, I'm panicky.

Don't leave me alone.

"Wait," I call out, without even meaning to.

He stops, but doesn't turn around.

"Yes?"

"Will you be at dinner tonight?"

My question is breathless and I internally kick myself. *Stop acting so eager. You're sending mixed signals.* But my heart is mixed and I can't help it.

Dare starts walking again.

"Of course."

I watch him walk away, the way his broad shoulders and slim hips move.

He's everything to me, everything I've ever wanted and *ever will want.*

It makes me want to scream in frustration, because is there really something so bad about him that I should be pushing him away?

My heart thumps and I think there is... I just can't put my finger on it.

Yet.

Dare disappears over the hill towards the house, and it's a few seconds before I realize that I'm being watched.

The tiny hairs stand up on my neck, and goose-bumps form on my arms. I look around, scanning my surroundings, but no one is here.

I'm alone.

Or am I?

It seems... it seems... it seems like there is someone standing at the edge of the house. There is a movement, and was that a flash of gray? But then it's not there and I'm imagining it.

For a moment, as I'm dwarfed by the shadows, and as the silence envelops me, I feel more alone than I've ever felt in my life.

It's not a good feeling.

It's actually terrifying.

St. Michael save me.

Save me.

Save me.

My fingers find Finn's necklace, buried under my shirt. I grasp it in my fingers, as I pray to the archangel.

St. Michael, protect me.

Protect me from the snares of the devil, because somehow I know the devil is here.

He's here and I'm in danger.

I just don't know what the danger is.

But you do.

Protect me til I know.

Protect me.

Protect me.

Protect me.

Chapter Six

There is a whispering in the hall, and I pull on my clothes, eager to leave this room behind. I throw open my doors to find Sabine in the hall, speaking with Jones.

They both look up at me, surprised at my abrupt appearance.

"Can we help you, Miss Price?" Jones asks, his tone so formal and stiff.

He belongs here, I think. *Here in this stiff, stiff house.*

"No, thank you," I say. "I'm just restless."

Sabine notices the book beneath my arm.

"We have a magnificent library here," she tells me. "Come with me and I'll show you."

We pass through the quiet halls and the silent rooms, and always, always, always, I feel watched. Invisible eyes stare through me, into me, and I hate it.

There is something here.

Something.

"Do you feel safe here?" I ask her abruptly as she pushes open the library doors. She turns to me, surprised.

"Of course, Miss Price," she says throatily. "You don't?"

"Please, call me Calla," I tell her, avoiding the question as she leads me into the room.

Shelves of books surround me, lining the room, ceiling to floor.

"I'll light the fireplace to get rid of the morning chill," she says, crossing the room and kneeling in front of the beautiful stone.

I leave her as quickly as I can, to get away from her question, and I go from book to book, but of course she doesn't forget and when I turn back around, she's there.

"Let's sit by the fire, child."

It's a suggestion, but she's pulling my elbow and so I find myself beside the lapping flames. She sits next to me, and her gaze is magnetic.

"Why do you feel unsafe here," she asks. "Has something happened?"

My brother and mother died.

That's what I want to say.

But I don't because that's awkward, and so I swallow hard instead.

"Do you feel guilty for surviving?" she asks, her words direct and insightful.

I swallow again.

"Because things happen for a reason, the way they're meant to happen. You survived them because you were meant to. There is no guilt in that."

"I miss them," I whisper. And it feels like a confession. I always felt I had to be strong for dad, to not show weakness. To hold up Finn.

But Finn wasn't real.

He was gone all along.

I don't have to be strong anymore.

Sabine nods and she gazes into the flames.

"I know," she says. "I didn't know your brother, but I miss your mother. She used to brighten my days, child. Whitley can be dark. Your mama was a light."

For some reason, her words only make me sadder because that light has been snuffed, and there's only darkness here now.

The fire warms my knees and my bones, and I cup my hands to my chest. I block out my emotions, because emotions only hurt.

Instead, I want to know about Dare.

"Dare grew up here?" I ask, trying to sound casual. "He must've been a light for you, too."

Although even now those words sound ridiculous. Dare is beautiful, Dare is my heart, but Dare isn't a light.

He's my darkness.

Sabine smiles and her smile is sad.

"Dare did grow up here," she confirms. "He was mine, as much as Laura was. He still is, child. I couldn't help him once, but I'd protect him now with my life."

She looks at me now defensively, as though she has to protect him from *me*.

I'm confused, and I want to ask why, but I can't.

Because Dare himself finds us.

"Sabby," he says as he crosses the room, but his eyes are on me. "Jones needs you."

She stares at him knowingly. He has come to save me once again, to rescue me from this situation and Sabine knows it. She creaks out of the chair and shuffles away.

She doesn't look back.

"She loves you," I offer, without looking up.

The flames are red and they lick at me.

"Yes," he agrees simply and he takes her vacant seat.

He takes my book from my hands, staring at the cover.

"Jane Eyre," he observes and he sifts through the pages. "Interesting choice. Are you my Jane, Calla?"

I swallow and look away.

Because that would make him Mr. Rochester.

"Jane saved Rochester, you know," Dare continues, his voice smooth like the night. "Eventually."

"I can't save anyone," I tell him helplessly. "Because I don't know all the facts."

Dare closes his eyes and he seems to glow from the flames.

"You do."

I just can't remember them.

He opens his eyes again, and the expression knifes me in the heart, because I've seen it before.

It's hurt, it's vulnerable, it's anxious.

It's hiding something.

Something I know.

Something that scares me.

Save me, and I'll save you.

"I don't like it here," I murmur.

"I know."

***

I write my dad a letter, and I give it to Sabine.

"He'll want to know I'm ok," I tell her. She nods because of course he will.

She hands me a cup of tea.

In England, tea fixes everything.

"Is Dare here?" I ask casually, because even now, he's the sun and I'm the moon. I need his light to live.

She shakes her head. "No. He'll be back though, child. He always comes back."

What a strange thing to say.

But I don't dwell on it.

Instead, I think about light.

I think about how the moonlight is really a reflection of the sun, of how the moon doesn't create any light at all. So a thing that seems to radiate silvery, ethereal light is really the darkest of the dark.

I'm the moon.

And I have no light of my own.

I need Dare for that.

But if he's the sun, he'll burn me.

And my metaphors are making me sick.

I retreat to the gardens, where I'm surrounded by flowers and silence.

All I have are my thoughts here, and my mind is a scary place.

I close my eyes and will my memories to return,

But all I can see is the past.

The past I know.

Not the things that I don't.

My mother's screams haunt me.

Finn's headstone, my tears.

His journal, which I left at home.

I wish I'd brought it.

At least I'd feel closer to him, even though his words were crazy.

I picture a page filled with scribble, with his familiar handwriting and scratched out words.

With perfect clarity, I remember it.

Calla will save me.

Or I will die.

I will die.

I will die.

Serva me, serva bo te.

Save me and I'll save you.

A shudder runs through me because I couldn't.

I couldn't save Finn.

And no amount of words and consolation… from my father, from Dare, from Sabine… no amount of argument can change that.

You survived them for a reason.

Sabine's nonsense comes back to me, and I ponder it.

For *what* reason?

I don't know.

Is my reason to save Dare, like Jane saved Mr. Rochester?

I don't know.

All I know is I have to uncover his truth if I am ever to save anything.

The truth will set us all free.

Chapter Seven

I'm lost again.

Whitley is so large that I find I'm perpetually lost. Somehow, I find myself outside of Eleanor's study today, and I hear her voice coming from within.

Reaching out to grip the doorknobs, I pause because she doesn't seem happy. With the door already cracked, I can hear the words loud and clear.

"She's not well, Eleanor," Sabine says in her creaky voice. "She needs rest and solitude, I fear."

"Then she'll get it here at Whitley," Eleanor says impatiently. "I don't see the reason for your concern."

"She's lost everything," Sabine offers. "And you don't offer her anything but shelter. Perhaps if you would just tell her…"

"Tell her what?" Eleanor snaps. "Remind her that…"

"Haven't you heard it's impolite to eavesdrop?"

Dare steps around me, studying me curiously. He's handsome, he's enigmatic, he's in my personal space. He also doesn't want me to hear what they're saying.

I take a breath. "What is everyone hiding from me?" I ask him bluntly.

He shakes his head. "It's nothing."

It's everything. I feel it.

"I need to know," I insist. He stares at me.

"You're here to recover, Calla. To rest, to come back to yourself..."

"But you said that I'm not safe," I remind him. "Shouldn't I know from what?"

He's uncomfortable now, and his dark eyes seem to shimmer. "So much has happened to this family. You don't need to think about it right now. You're just going to have to trust me."

I wish I could.

"This is madness," I whisper.

"We're all a bit mad, I suppose," he quotes Lewis Carroll for what, I assume, is a lack of a better answer. My fingernails dig into my palm because I'm so frustrated.

"I love you, you know," he offers, and his face is suddenly gentle. "God, I hate this, Calla."

He walks away, like standing near me is painful.

I do the only thing I can do. I retreat to my room, where I'm alone and no one is watching. The room is lonely and quiet, and I can't take the silence.

"Finn, you'd hate this place."

Of course there's no answer, but it makes me feel better to talk to him, to pretend my other half is still living, still making me whole.

I picture his face and he laughs.

"You're such a goof, Cal," he tells me, his pale blue eyes twinkling. "You were always the better half. You don't need me."

"That's dumb," I reply instantly. "I'll always need you. I'm probably going to never stop talking to you, ok?"

He rolls his eyes and stands in the moonlight. "Fine. But there's going to come a time when I stop answering. Because eventually, you have to let me go, Cal. For your own good."

"Don't tell me what my own good is," I scowl, but he laughs, because that's what Finn does. He laughs and he makes every situation better.

"Stay with me," I urge him. "I feel so alone."

He nods and he sits on the bed with me, and he watches me while I settle down to sleep. He hums, a song without words, a song that's familiar, but I can't place the name.

"Sleep," he tells me. "I'm right here."

So I do. I sleep while the memory of my dead brother watches over me, because that's the only way I feel safe.

But even then, my dreams plague me.

"One for one for one."

The whispers seem to come from the corners, from the shadows, from the halls. "One for one, Calla. One for me, one for me."

It cackles and hisses and I run around the corners, into the dark.

As I escape, I realize something and skid to a halt.

I left Finn behind.

They have him now.

No.

No.

I have to go back. I turn, but I can't move. My feet are enmeshed with the ground.

I hear him screaming and I force myself to move, but I'm suddenly stopped by Dare.

He grabs my arms and restrains me, his arms like steel bands, not letting me go.

"You can't help him now," he tells me somberly, his black eyes glistening. "I'm sorry."

My screams wake me up and Finn is still sitting on the side of my bed.

"Are you ok?" My brother's voice is anxious, and the moonlight shines onto his face. "You're just having a dream. Wake up, it's ok."

I nod and grab his hand and he grins.

"Was it the bogeyman?"

I try to smile back, but the feeling of terror and loss is still too great.

I nod instead. "Yeah. The bogeyman."

It's a private joke, because Finn and I have always said that there's no bogeyman in the entire world that we're scared of since we sleep in a funeral home.

But my dream…. It preyed on the thing that *does* scare me, the thing that has always scared me the most.

Losing my brother.

But that already happened, and I survived, and I'm still here.

But the fear still owns me, because I can't let him go.

"I'm fine," I tell him confidently. Because it was just a dream.

Just a dream. The worst already happened.

He nods and starts to get up, but I tug at his hand. "Stay."

Because maybe it was a dream, but it was so real.

There is understanding in my brother's eyes and he curls up next to me without a word. There are no words needed, just his soothing presence. Real or not, he calms me and I'm not ready to give that up.

It's not long before Finn's breathing is soft and even and I know I've imagined him into sleep.

I watch him, the way his chest pulls deep breaths, the way his mouth is slack. The way he's my other half and I have no idea what I'll do without him, even though I know I have to try.

My chest is still aching from the dream, my heart still skipping beats. I've never had such a real nightmare before. It rattled me to my core.

It made me never want to sleep again, for fear of having the same dream again.

So I climb from my bed and roam the halls of Whitley.

Something about this house disturbs me. It's as though there is darkness in its heart, as though it has a soul, and it wants to absorb mine. I realize just how crazy my thoughts are, and I fight to suppress them.

Treading lightly, I quietly pad over the marble until I get to the massive glass doors of the library.

I only hesitate a moment before I open them and head outside.

I don't know why.

I just know that I need some air. I need to be away from the pressing confines of the house. Something in here stifles me.

It's not until I'm halfway down the path to the stables that I realize I'm barefoot. I'd walked from the house without any shoes.

What kind of lunatic am I?

I'm just turning to go back to the house when two headlights appear down the driveway. They shine into me, illuminating me through my nightgown, exposing my every line and curve. I wrap my arms around my waist, attempting to conceal myself in vain. But the car, a dark Porsche, doesn't stop. It rolls past me toward the garage, and as it passes, Dare's dark eyes stare at me through the driver's window.

It must be 3 am and he's only just now getting home?

Where in the world has he been?

But with a sinking heart, I know that it's not my business, because I told him I wanted space. Because he's an adult and he can come and go as he pleases and this is what I wanted.

It starts to rain so I pick up the pace, but it's a wasted effort. By the time I make it to the gardens, it's pouring, and I have to stop in a gazebo to wait it out. The wet winds blow across the moors, howling in a hauntingly chilling moan, and chills run up and down my spine.

I'd thought living in a funeral home was creepy. This estate makes that seem like child's play.

Shivering, I huddle under the roof, the wind cutting through my wet nightgown.

What was I thinking coming out here?

"You know, most people wear shoes. And clothes."

Dare lunges beneath the roof for shelter, soaked from head to toe. Unlike me, he's fully clothed, but exactly like me, he's completely wet.

"It's not doing you a lot of good," I point out. "You're soaked through."

He shrugs as he leans against a column, barely out of the downpour, shaking the water from his hair. He's long and slim, and something about him reminds me of a deadly cobra, coiled to strike.

"It's ok. I won't melt, trust me."

He examines me, his eyes as black as night. "What are you doing out here in the middle of the night, anyway?"

I think I see amusement in his eyes, amusement laced with concern, but I look away before I can be sure. This situation unsettles me, puts me on edge...wakes up every nerve ending.

"I couldn't sleep."

I don't see the need to tell him that I *was* sleeping, but that a bad dream starring him woke me. No one needs to know that.

"You should go see Sabine tomorrow," he tells me, his words helpful but his tone bored. "She's a master at herbs. She's got a tea that will put you down for the count."

Somehow, that doesn't surprise me. Sabine, with her tiny twisted body and her dark mysterious eyes... it seems right that she would dabble in herbs.

"Ok. Maybe I will."

Dare studies me, his eyes sweeping me from head to toe, watching my teeth chatter for a couple of minutes.

"If I had a jacket, I'd offer it to you."

His words are quiet in the night, and offering a jacket is such a gentlemanly thing to do.

"Don't look so surprised," he chuckles. "I may not be as nice as you, but I have manners." He straightens his body out, opening his arms. "Come here, Calla."

To his warmth.

To his strength.

I want to.

I want to.

But I shake my head, determined.

Dare's eyes cloud, and his arms drop back to his sides.

He pushes away from the column and approaches me, his long body lithe and slender. I gulp hard as he steps toward me, closer, then closer.

For a brief moment, I feel like prey and he's the hunter, until reality hits me and I know that he would never want to hunt me. I'm night and he's day. He's whole and I'm broken.

"You're going to catch your death out here," he tells me, his voice gentle now, and this whole 'I need space' thing is killing me, killing me, killing me.

I wonder if it's killing him, too?

"Come on, follow me," he tells me, pushing ahead. For some reason, I do as he asks and I allow him to lead me through the gardens, up the paths, into the house and to a huge laundry room. He opens a cabinet and pulls out a large soft towel. As he turns to me, he pulls it around my shoulders.

"You're not used to the rain here," he tells me as he rubs my arms briskly. "Don't go out at night again. You don't know what's out there."

I don't bother to remind him that Oregon rain is just as bad, that both places are wet and gray and dreary, and that I'm used to it. I don't ask him what's out there, because I don't want to know. Not yet.

"I... um." I fall silent. "Why are you being so nice?" I blurt. "I'm not being very nice to *you.*"

"You're doing what you have to do," he tells me, a strange look in his dark eyes. "Things aren't what they seem here, Calla. Don't forget that and you'll be fine."

And with that, he walks out, leaving me alone in the room with a wet towel in my hand.

I make my way back to my room, through the quiet halls, and as I pass the windows, it feels like something growls.

Something waits,

Something sleeps in the dark.

I don't know what it is.

But it knows *me.*

Of that, I am certain.

Chapter Eight

I'm so lonely.

I know I'm here to mend, to fix what's broken, to remember what I forgot.

But being alone is lonely.

I write my dad another letter, and give it to Sabine.

I'm fine, I assured him in print. I lied but maybe he won't know that.

If Whitley holds any answers, I certainly haven't found them yet.

Picking up my medallion, I find myself whispering.

"St. Michael, protect me. Protect me from what I don't know. Guide me to what I need to find."

I drop the necklace back into my shirt, and the metal is cold on my skin. The coolness reminds me of Finn, of how he isn't alive, and I'm devastated all over again.

Every time I remember, it rips the band-aid off.

Being without him is excruciating, and it hits me at the strangest times.

There are hours until dinner, so I creep through the halls, intent on distracting myself, on discovering something. *Anything.*

I find an old nursery, with two bassinets and a creepy rocking horse. Its wooden eye watches me lifelessly as I idly stare around the room.

The walls are pale yellow and old, the floor is gleaming hardwood, the ceilings are high. There are chandeliers even in here, in a place where children were supposed to flourish.

But the toys are scarce and the formality is abundant.

The silence is unnerving.

A nursery without babies is haunting.

"This was your mother's nursery," Sabine says from behind me. "And your uncle's."

"Were they close in age?" I ask because I know nothing of my own family.

She nods. "But they weren't close. Dickie was troubled and your mother was not. Are you homesick, child?"

Of course I am.

And of course I'm not.

Home was frightening.

But I still miss it.

The nanny smiles, her teeth dark.

"Come with me, then," she urges, and I do.

We climb into an old pick-up truck and we drive for what seems like hours.

But eventually, eventually, we pull to a stop and we're by the coast, and the sun sparkles on the water.

I peer into it, and I'm unprepared for the relief that flushes through me at the sight of the sand and the water.

"It looks a bit like the pictures your mother sent me," Sabine says quietly. "From your home in America. These are the Seven Sisters Cliffs, and I thought you might like it here." She hands me a basket, containing a blanket, my book, and some water.

"I have shopping to do at a few local farms. I'll be back here in a couple of hours to retrieve you."

I nod, touched by her thoughtfulness, and guilty that I hadn't expected it from her. Her truck leaves me alone, and I'm so small next to the ocean.

I walk up and down the beach, my feet sinking in the damp sand.

The foam slides back and forth and I skirt it, heading away from it to the jagged white edges of the cliffs.

I'm at home here in this rugged place.

I'm at home on the edge, where any minute I can fall.

I climb and climb, and when I'm on top, I stare down at the world.

I'm big and it's small, and the ocean is my buffer.

I spread my blanket, and open my book, and I lose myself in it.

I lose myself in a world that isn't mine and for a while, that's for the best.

I suck in my breath at the end, when Jane finally saves Mr. Rochester.

She saves him from loneliness and despair.

Is that what Dare needs saving from?

I drop the book in the basket and lift my face to the sun.

It bakes me, warms me, soothes me.

It's when my eyes are closed that I see them.

The visions.

The memories.

Finn shouts.

Glass breaks.

Tires skid.

The water pounds the shore.

Metal bends and shrieks.

"Are you ok?" Dare asks, and his voice is afraid.

He wasn't supposed to be there.

I can't get away from that fact.

But I can't, for the life of me, figure it out.

I can't come to the truth.

A wall stands in my mind, blocking me,

Protecting me.

But I can't be protected forever.

I have to tell you something.

It's new.

A new memory.

From before the accident.

I startle, and focus.

Calla, I have to tell you something. You won't understand. Please just listen before you decide I'm a monster.

My breath… it won't come, and I try and try to inhale, and I try and try to remember more.

But that's all.

Dare's face is gone.

He's afraid he's a monster, and maybe he is.

I don't know.

But being here, in the wind and the air, perhaps even at Whitley, is freeing me to remember. Everyone was right, the answers are here.

I feel it.

I just don't like it.

The water crashes below me and it's like a lullaby or a song, until it turns into sort of a snarl…then my name.

Calla.

It's a whisper carried on the wind.

I open my eyes, and someone is staring at me.

The boy in the hood.

He's on the edge of the water, his feet buried in the foam, and I can't see his eyes.

I hesitate, then lift my hand.

He's in my mind.

But why?

Is he a memory?

He cocks his head and I'm not afraid, and then he walks away into the sunlight.

Chapter Nine

"Calla!"

It's Dare shouting, and when I look, he's standing below on the beach.

His pants are rolled up and there is sun in his hair.

I smile before I can stop myself,

Because even though I shouldn't,

I want him.

I want him now.

I want him always.

He climbs to me and sits on the blanket and when he stares at me, his gaze is black.

"Sabine sent me," he explains. "She's going to be late and didn't want you here alone."

I nod, and I'm so thankful he's here, because I'm tired of being alone.

My mind is a deep ocean and I'm drowning.

"You were afraid I'd think you're a monster," I tell him softly, and I watch his face carefully. His mouth tightens, but that's his only reaction.

"Yes. Do you remember why?"

I sift a handful of sand through my fingers, watching each tiny piece.

"No. Not yet."

He sighs and it's loud up here, on the top of this cliff by the sea.

"Where should I look for the answers?" I ask him, and I hear the desperation in my voice because I'm tired of the unrest.

I'm tired of the secrets.

I'm tired of nothing being clear.

He blinks.

"You should look at Whitley," he finally says. "But you've got to be careful. You won't like what you find.'

I nod because I know I won't.

Because it might make me think Dare's a monster.

He holds my hand as we walk to his car, and I let him.

Because I need his light to live,

Because a monster lives in us all.

That's what I tell Finn later when I'm alone in my room.

My brother stares at me with imaginary pale blue eyes.

"Maybe,' he muses. "But that doesn't take away the fact that Dare was on our mountain that night, Calla."

"The night you died," I nod. He looks away and I know he doesn't like being dead.

"*Was* he there?" Finn asks, and I can tell from his tone, that he knows. "Or are you confused?"

I sigh, long and loud, because I'm so tired of being the only one hidden from the truth.

"Just tell me," I demand.

"I can't." His answer is simple.

"But you want to."

"Yes."

He gets up and paces the room, a slender lion in a cage. "Think, Calla. You know this one."

I do.

I do know it.

It's on the tip of my mind, dying to find its way in.

I close my eyes.

I spoke to Dare that night. I can hear his words.

Anxious, afraid.

Concentrating, I see the cliffs, the funeral home, the moon.

I see my brother,

And he's alive,

Then he's not.

My mother,

My father,

The flashing lights.

The beach.

And then…

There's something.

A flicker.

I crane my neck, trying to see more.

VERUM

A flash of dark hair,
And a name.
I open my eyes.
"Who's Olivia?" I ask limply.
Finn smiles.
"Now we're getting somewhere."

Chapter Ten

If I stay inside too long, the walls start closing in on me.

I hate the silence, I hate the height of the ceilings, I hate that I'm alone.

I hate that I long to call Dare, to tell him to find me in this Godforsaken place, to take me away...because to be honest, I don't really have anywhere to go.

I can't go home.

I can't face it without Finn.

But God knows I can't stay in this house.

The breeze is slightly chilly as I make my way deep into the grounds. I've come to believe that it never truly warms up here. The rain makes the lawns lush, though. Green and full and colorful. As Finn would've said in his endless quest to learn Latin... it's viridem. And green means life.

The cobbled path turns to pebbles as I get further away from the house, and after a minute, I come to a literal fork in the road. The path splits into two. One leads towards a wooded area, and the other leads to a beautiful stone building on the edge of the horizon, shrouded in mist and weeping trees.

It's small and mysterious, beautiful and ancient. And of course I have to get a closer look. Without a second thought, I head down that path.

The closer I get, the more my curiosity grows.

I can smell the moss as I approach, that musty, dank smell that comes with a closed room or a wet space. And with that dark scent comes a very oppressive feeling. I feel it weighing on my shoulders as I open the heavy door, as I stare at the word SAVAGE inscribed in the wood, as I take my first tentative step into a room that hasn't seen human life in what looks like years.

But it *has* seen death.

I'm standing in a mausoleum.

Growing up in a funeral home, I'm well versed in death. I know what it looks like, what it smells like, even what it tastes like in the air.

I'm surrounded by it here.

The floor is stone, but since it is deprived of light, soft green moss grows in places, and is soft under my feet. The walls are thick blocks of stone, and have various alcoves, filled with the remains of Savage family members. They go back for generations, and it makes me wonder how long the Savages have lived at Whitley.

Nearest me, are Richard Savage I, my grandfather, and Richard Savage II, my uncle. And next to him is Olivia.

Olivia.

The name from my memory.

Dare's mother.

I run my fingers along her name, tracing the letters cut in the stone, absorbing the coolness, the hardness.

What do I know about her?

Why is she significant in my memory?

Did Dare have her eyes, or her hair? Was she the only spot of brightness in his world? Does he miss her more than life itself?

I don't know.

All I know is her name was in my head yesterday…before I found this place.

It's my first hard clue.

Trailing my fingers along the wall, I circle the room, eyeing my ancestors, marveling at the silence here.

It's so loud that my ears ring with it.

The open door creates a sliver of light on the dark floor, and it's while I'm focusing on the brightness that I first hear the whisper.

Calla.

I whip my head around, only to find nothing behind me.

Chills run down my spine, and goose-bumps form on my arms as I eye the empty room. The only people here are dead.

But... the whisper was crystal clear in the silence.

I'm hearing voices.

That fact terrifies me, but not as much as the familiarity in that whisper.

It can't be my brother.

It can't. He's dead and I know it. I might've imagined him the other night, but even I know he wasn't real.

"Hello?" I call out, desperate for someone to be here, for someone real to have spoken. But no one answers.

Of course not.

I'm alone.

I lay my hand on the wall and try to draw in a deep breath. I can't be crazy. It's one of my worst fears, second only to losing my brother.

A movement catches my eye and I focus on it.

Carnation petals and stargazers, white and red, blow across the floor. Funeral flowers.

Startled, I turn toward them, bending to touch them. I run one between my fingers, its texture velvety smooth. It hadn't been here a moment ago. None of them had, but yet here they are, strewn across the floor.

They lead to a crypt in the wall.

Adair Phillip DuBray.

My heart pounds and pounds as I race to the plaque, as I trace the fresh letters with my fingertips.

This hadn't been here either.

What the hell?

I gulp, drawing in air, observing the fresh flowers in the vase beside his name.

There is no moss here, because this had been freshly carved, recently opened, and very recently sealed. But there's no way Dare can be here, because I just saw him last night. He's fine, he's fine, he's fine.

As my hands palm his name, as I reassure myself, pictures fill my head, images and smells.

The sea, a cliff, a car.

Blood, shrieking metal, the water.

Dare.

He's bloody,

He's bloody,

He's bloody.

Everything is on fire,

The flames lick at the stone walls,

Trying to find any possible way out.

The smoke chokes me and I cough,

gasping for air.

I blink and everything is gone.

My hands are on a blank wall, and Dare's name is gone.

The flowers are gone.

I'm alone.

The floor is bare.

I can't breathe.

I can't breathe.

I can't breathe.

I'm crazy.

It's the only explanation.

I scramble for the door and burst out into the sunlight, away from the mausoleum, away from the death. I fly toward the house, tripping on the stones.

"Calla?"

My name is called and I'm afraid to look, afraid no one will be there, afraid that I'm still imagining things. Is this what Finn felt like every day? Am I starting down that slippery path? It's a rabbit hole and I'm the rabbit and I'm crazy.

But it's Dare, standing tall and strong on the path, and I fly into his arms, without worrying about pushing him away.

His arms close around me and he smells so good, so familiar, and I close my eyes.

"You're fine," I tell him, I tell myself. "You're ok."

"Yeah, I'm fine," he says in confusion, his hands stroking my back, holding me close. "Did you think something happened?"

I see his name, carved in the mausoleum stone, and I shudder, pushing the vision away, far out of my mind.

"No. I...no."

He holds me for several minutes more, then looks down at me, tucking an errant strand of my hair behind my ear.

"Are you ok? You've been gone for hours."

Hours? How can that be? The sky swirls, and I steady myself against his chest.

I hear his heart and it's beating fast, because he's afraid.

He's afraid for me because he recognizes the signs, he's seen them before.

"It's ok, Cal," he murmurs, but I can hear the concern in his voice. "It's ok."

But I can tell from his voice that it's not.

Craziness is genetic.

I'm the rabbit.

And I'm crazy.

Dare's arm is around my shoulders as we walk back to the house, and I can feel him glance at me from time to time.

"Stop," I tell him finally as we walk through the gardens. "I'm fine."

"Ok," he agrees. "Of course you are."

But he knows better, and he knows that I'm not.

Sabine is kneeling by the library doors, digging through the rich English soil, and she looks at us over her shoulder. When she sees my face, her eyes narrow and she climbs to her feet.

"Are you all right, Miss Price?" she asks in her gravelly voice. I want to lie, I want to tell her that I'm fine, but I know she can tell the difference. In fact, as she stares at me with those dark eyes, I feel like she can see into my soul.

I don't bother to lie.

I just shake my head.

She nods.

"Come with me."

She leads us both to the back of the house, to her room. It's small and dark, draped in colorful fabrics, in mystic symbols and pieces of gaudy jewelry, shrouded in mirrors and dream-catchers and stars.

I'm stunned and I pause, gazing at all of the pageantry.

She glimpses my expression and shrugs. "I'm Rom," she says, by way of explanation. At my blank expression, she sighs. "Romani. Gypsy. I'm not ashamed of it."

She holds her head up high, her chin out, and I can see that she's far from ashamed. She's proud.

"You shouldn't be," I assure her weakly. "It's your heritage. It's fascinating."

She's satisfied by that, by the idea that I'm not looking down at her for who she is.

Her dark eyes tell a story, and to me, they tell me that she knows more than I do. That she might even know more about *me* than I do.

It's crazy, I know.

But apparently, I'm crazy now.

Sabine guides me to a velvet chair and pushes me gently into it. She glances at Dare.

"Leave us," she tells him softly. "I've got her now. She'll be fine."

He's hesitant and he looks at me, and I nod.

I'll be fine.

I think.

He slips away.

Sabine rustles about and as she does, I look around. On the table next to me, tarot cards are splayed out, formed in an odd formation, as though I'd interrupted a fortune telling.

I gulp because something hangs in the air here.

Something mystical.

After a minute, Sabine shoves a cup into my hands.

"Drink. It's lemon balm and chamomile. It'll settle your stomach and calm you down."

I don't bother to ask how she knew I was upset. It must've been written all over my face.

I sip at the brew and after a second, she glances at me.

"Better?"

I nod. "Thank you."

She smiles and her teeth are scary. I look away, and she roots through a cabinet. She extracts her prize and hands me a box.

"Take this at night. It'll help you sleep." I glance at her questioningly, and she adds, "Dare told me."

I take the box, which is unmarked, and she nods. "Your mama used to have trouble sleeping. And she had bouts of nerves, too."

Sabine has no way of knowing that my 'bout of nerves' included hallucinations and hearing voices, so I just smile and thank her.

I glance at her table again. "Are you a fortune-teller, Sabine?" It feels odd to say those words in a serious manner, but the old woman doesn't miss a beat.

"I read the cards," she nods. "Someday, I'll read yours."

I don't know if I want to know what they'll say.

"Have you read Dare's?" I ask impulsively, and I don't know why. Sabine glances at me, her black eyes knowing.

"That boy doesn't need his fortune told. He writes his own."

I have no idea what that means, but I nod like I do.

"You'll be ok now," she tells me, her expression wise and I find myself believing her. She's got a calming nature, something that settles the air around her. I hadn't noticed that before.

"My mother never mentioned you," I murmur as I get to my feet. "I find that odd, since she must've loved you."

Sabine looks away. "Your mother doesn't have happy memories from here," she says quietly. "But I know her heart."

"Ok," I say uncertainly, as I hover over the threshold. Sabine lays her hand on my shoulder.

"If you need me again, you know where to find me."

I nod, and then I walk away. I feel Sabine staring at me as I do, but I resist the urge to turn around.

Instead, I focus on how much better Sabine made me feel, how much calmer.

Maybe the tea had valium in it.

As I walk into my room, I've decided that I must've imagined the whole thing. I haven't been sleeping well. My mind was playing tricks on me, as minds are prone to do when they're sleep deprived.

Obviously.

That's the explanation.

I raise my hand to tuck my hair behind my ear, and that's when I freeze.

My fingers smell like carnations and stargazers.

Chapter Eleven

Ropes bind me, holding me down, restraining me, biting into me.

I twist and turn, but there's no getting away from them.

My mind spirals, splinters, fractures, bursting into a million confused pieces.

Light gets in, illuminating, but there's no truth here. There is only nonsense and puzzles.

I can't understand,
And
I'm
Not
Sure
I
Want
To.

"Help!" I call out. But my voice echoes down hallways and corridors and rooms. No one is here but me, and I'm alone, and that's my worst fear.

"Someone!" my voice cracks and my fingers dig into the frayed rope. No one is there, but the rope breaks suddenly, throwing me against the wall with the force of my own movement.

I jump up to run, but then realize…

There's nowhere to go.

I sit in front of Eleanor's massive desk, uncomfortably waiting for her to speak. It's been a full twenty-four hours since I imagined the scene in the crypts. I've had time to wrap my mind around the hallucinations, and accept them for what they were: a product of sleeplessness. I'm ignoring the very real fact that my fingers had a distinct scent of roses on them that I couldn't have imagined.

Now I'm just waiting to hear Eleanor's expectations from me.

Regardless of what they consider to be my 'fragile state', there's apparently still a small matter of my inheritance to consider.

She stares at me for several moments before she begins, her voice stern and rigid.

"I trust you've settled in."

It's not a pleasantry, it's a directive.

I nod in response, as expected.

"Good. We have matters to discuss now, and I require your full attention."

I feel my spine, ram-rod straight, and I picture the vertebrae, lining up, afraid to slump in Eleanor's presence. I have to believe that the sun is afraid to shine with her around. She's that intimidating.

"I realize you aren't feeling well, and that is to be expected," Eleanor's British accent is thick, and I find myself distracted by that, and the fact that my mother lost her own over the years.

"But you have a significant inheritance from your grandfather," she continues, staring a hole into me. "And you must comply with certain stipulations in order to receive it. Since you are eighteen now, time is getting away from us."

"What are the stipulations?" I ask politely, and I itch to get out of this room.

Eleanor looks down her nose.

"First, you will attend Cambridge University. Every Savage has attended Cambridge, always. You will live here at Whitley during your University years."

Pause.

"You will submit to having me on your bank account, in addition to yourself."

Pause.

"You will work with my PR person to ensure you don't tarnish the Savage name."

Pause.

She looks me in the eye. "You will hyphenate your name. From here forward, you will be known as Price-Savage."

This last one gives me pause, because I know my father won't like it.

"Does Dare have to hyphenate his name, too?" I ask without thinking. Eleanor looks like she swallowed a lemon, her mouth pinching into a knot.

"Of course not. Adair is not a Savage, and never has been. His inheritance is a pittance compared to yours."

That doesn't seem quite fair.

I swallow hard.

"Lastly, and most importantly, you have until you turn nineteen to claim it. You must be of sound mind, Calla."

You must pull yourself together. That's what she's really saying. *You must not be crazy.*

I stare blankly at her.

"Are these terms agreeable to you?"

Eleanor waits, expecting me to agree, expecting me to make excuses for my frail mind. I don't. I finally answer with soft words.

"I'll try."

Eleanor is unflinching.

"Very well. You may go."

She looks down at her desk, her attention already on something else.

I let myself out, and when I'm in the hall, I allow Finn to join me.

"She can't be serious," he rolls his eyes.

I slump against the wall. "I'm afraid she is. I don't think she knows how to joke."

"I'm not changing my name," Finn tells me stoutly. "I'm a Price."

"She's not asking *you* to change it," I reply diplomatically. "You're dead. She's asking me. But not to change it, only to hyphenate it."

"Dad will have kittens," Finn points out, and I know he's right.

"Probably."

He chews his lip.

"But maybe. We'll think on it."

Like always, he speaks of us as a unit. Because we are, even now, even though he's dead.

"I need some things," I tell him. "Toiletry items," I add before he can ask. "Girl stuff. I think I'll go into town and pick them up. Do you want to come?"

He shakes his head. "For girl stuff? Uh, no. I think I'll just stay here and take an imaginary walk through the gardens."

"Good idea. I should practice being alone."

"You should," he nods, and I once again ponder my ridiculousness. Am I so pathetic that I have to imagine a reality?

Apparently, I am.

I find Jones downstairs, and hesitantly, I approach the imposing man.

"Is there any way you could take me into town? I need to go to the store."

"Of course, Miss Price," he nods, immediately interrupting what he's doing to tend to me. "I'll bring the car around."

I'm waiting out front when Dare comes out the door, breathtakingly sexy in a black outfit, black slacks and snug black shirt. He blows out of the house like a breeze, and stops next to me.

"Can I catch a ride with you?" he asks, eyeing me up and down, checking for weakness.

"Of course. But don't you drive?" I ask dumbly, because he's been driving himself somewhere every night. He cocks his head.

"Sometimes, I just wanna be lazy."

"Understandable," I nod. "You can by all means share my ride."

He leans against the house.

"Is your room comfortable?" he asks knowingly, because he has to know that it is. The politeness between us hurts me, it cuts like a knife and I want to yank it away.

But I can't.

The more distance between us, the safer I am.

I don't know how I know it, I just do.

I nod, and Dare smiles as the car glides to a stop in front of us. He opens the door for me, because even though he's not as nice as me, he has manners.

"Good."

He slides in next to me, and his fingers wrap around mine. I pull them away.

"Dare... I..." I stare at him, steeling myself, resolving myself. "I need you to not be nice to me."

His eyes widen, then narrow.

"Why?"

"Because it'll be easier that way."

He shakes his head, annoyance in his eyes. "Easier for who? If you want to push me away, I'm not going to make it easy on you, Calla."

"Is *this* easy on me?"

By *this* I mean my life and he knows it. My mother died. My brother died. I'm away from my father, here at Whitley, and I feel in my heart that I can't trust Dare. He's hiding something from me.

Dare shakes his head. "No. But there's no reason to make it harder, Calla. Don't push me away. Just... don't. You're not the only one who is struggling."

His eyes are so pained, so haunted, so sad.

My eyes feel hot and I blink wetness away, my heart heavy.

"Can you tell me what it is that I don't know?"

Dare freezes, his hand on his leg.

"No."

"Then I can't trust you. You have a secret. And *I hate secrets*, Dare. You should understand why."

He clenches his jaw and looks out the window, and I turn the opposite way.

I ignore him, stare out the window at the English countryside as we drive into town.

"How far are we from London?" I call up to Jones.

"About an hour, miss."

Jones answers, and Dare doesn't look up from his phone.

"Too far away," he says without looking at me.

"Why do you say that?" I ask him. He doesn't bother answering, just stares even more intently at his phone.

"Rude," I mutter under my breath.

I think I see his lip twitch, but I can't be certain.

You wanted him to not be so nice.

He's taking me at my word.

It doesn't take long to get to the little town, and it takes even less time for Dare to get out of the car and start down the sidewalk, away from the car.

"We'll be back here in an hour," he calls over his shoulder to Jones.

How presumptuous.

"Will an hour be sufficient?" Jones asks me in his stiff voice. "I'll wait longer for you if necessary."

"I'm sure an hour will be fine," I assure him. He nods and I head toward the stores, but as I notice Dare duck from the main sidewalk onto an alley, my curiosity is piqued. I change course and follow him.

It's against my better judgment, but I can't help myself.

He moves fast, but I keep up.

We wind between buildings on the narrow alleyways, and I almost lose him twice, but manage to keep him in my sights. I watch his wide shoulders sway ahead of me, before he cuts down another side street.

I follow.

The alley grows narrow and dark, the cobblestones rough and uneven. I lose sight of Dare among the shadows, then I trip. As I fumble to steady myself, I suddenly find myself yanked against the wall.

Before I can breathe or scream, Dare's face materializes in front of me, as thunderous and dark as it is handsome.

"Hunting for something?" he asks bluntly, his voice sharp and low. His hands are on my shoulders, and I realize that I'm firmly pinned to the wall in front of him. He's not hurting me, he's just not letting me go.

I'm restrained beneath his palms.

I can feel his hips, I can feel his heat.

I can feel the part of him that makes him a man.

My own cheeks flush from it.

"No," I begin, then when he raises his eyebrows, I sigh. "Yes."

"What?" He doesn't release me.

"The truth," I tell him honestly.

"Have you ever heard the phrase *what you don't know might hurt you*?" Dare asks, his eyes laser sharp as he stares into mine.

I nod.

"Well, what you *do* know might hurt you too. Don't snoop. You probably won't like what you find. You have to let it come to you."

"I wasn't… I wasn't snooping," I manage to offer. "I don't know what I was doing."

Dare steps back, releasing me.

He's tall and slender and strong, and he makes me a bit breathless.

"That's probably your first issue," he tells me. "If you don't know what you're doing, you'll never get anywhere. Get out of this dark alley, Calla. It's not safe here."

He points at the entrance, and when he does, I see them.

The flowers he dropped on the ground.

Roses, stargazers and carnations.

My heart thuds and I do what I'm told. When I hit the sidewalk and emerge into the daylight, I turn, but he's already gone. So are the flowers.

I find the nearest shop, find my toiletry items and am back to the car well within the hour. I wait inside for Dare to return, and with each minute that passes, I wonder what I'll say to him.

But I don't have to decide.

Because finally Jones pokes his head into the back.

"Apparently, Mr. DuBray isn't coming right now. I'll come back for him later."

112

I nod silently and allow Jones to drive me back to Whitley.

Without even realizing it, I watch for the limo to go back out and return with Dare, but it never does. I don't know how Dare manages to get back home.

I know he does, though. Because in the middle of the night, I'm woken from a troubled sleep by a noise I can't define. I lay for a minute, trying to wake up enough to clear my mind, and I finally realize that it's piano music drifting through Whitley's halls.

I grab my robe and follow the haunting notes, finding myself in the salon.

I linger quietly in the massive doorway, watching Dare play the piano with the grace of a master. His long fingers drift across the keys and he stares out the window while he plays, his eyes absently watching the moors outside through the windows. The notes of the piano are haunting and low, delicate and high, and everywhere in between.

He doesn't know I'm here, and I want to keep it that way, because right now, while he thinks no one is watching, Dare DuBray looks absolutely and heart-wrenchingly vulnerable.

He looks open and casual, thoughtful and real.

It's the first real emotion I've seen on him.

It intrigues me, particularly since there isn't a trace of his trademark arrogance.

For a moment, I forget his rudeness from earlier. All I can think of is how very different he seems right now.

This is the person I love, the person I don't truly want to live without.

I'm so lost in my thoughts about him that I don't even realize that he's stopped playing. He's staring at me by the time I realize it, and the guard is back up in his eyes.

"Do you need something, or are you just taking a walk at 3 am?" he asks, his voice low and calm.

I shake my head. "No, I was just on my way to the kitchens."

"You must be turned around. They're on the opposite side of the house," he tells me evenly. *I'm busted.*

"Dare, what's your secret?"

Because I have to know.

He stares at the keys, at his hands that are playing them.

"I can't tell you."

I nod, because I was expecting that.

I turn around, but then I pause.

"You play beautifully."

He doesn't answer, and I walk away.

Chapter Twelve

Moonlight sweeps across the hallway, illuminating the heavy furniture and expensive rugs. I'm unfazed by it as I leave Dare at his piano and continue down the hall.

I need to know what is being hidden from me.

I feel like everyone knows it but me.

Dare.

Sabine.

My father.

Even Eleanor.

If I were hiding something here, where would I put it?

The answer is immediate.

Eleanor's office.

Surprisingly, it's unlocked and I quietly slip inside, treading across the thick rugs until I'm sitting in her large chair. From here, I feel like I'm at the helm of a ship, and I open the drawer next to my left leg. File folders line up, waiting for me to explore them, and I run my hands along their tops, hunting.

My fingers pause on D.

Dare DuBray.

I almost hesitate as I pull it out and open it, but then I feel no remorse. He knows everything about me. I might as well know something about him.

Adair Phillip DuBray.

6'2. Brown hair, brown eyes.

Mother, Olivia, deceased.

Father, Phillip, deceased.

Step-father, Richard II, deceased.

He's all alone. It hits me hard, because I know how that feels. His file is fairly short, and a few paragraphs have been redacted, two thick paragraphs with fat black lines drawn through them, preventing me from reading the words.

What is so bad that it can't be exposed in his file?

I'm confused and agitated, but then my eyes narrow as I come to the part that discusses his part of the Savage estate.

When Richard I died, he'd left the bulk of the estate to Calla Price (me!) and Finn Price, but there is a small trust to take care of Dare for the rest of his life. He would inherit more only if Finn or I are deemed incompetent, or die.

Apparently, Eleanor didn't inherit.

This shocks me to my core as I sit in her seat and imagine the way she looks so militant and in charge. She got nothing?

But I got… everything. Me and Finn.

Upon Finn's death, his share went to me, not to Dare.

Why?

I don't know how much it is worth, but judging by Whitley and the limousine, and the family business, Savage Inc, I know it must be worth a large fortune.

I'm worth a large fortune.

But only if I'm of sound mind.

Astounded, I slip the file back in, and I think I'm going to get up and leave when I see my name.

I yank the file out, wasting no time in examining it.

Calla Elizabeth Price.

Female twin to Finn. Red hair, blue eyes, 5'7". Dress size, six. Shoe size, eight. Attended public high school at Astoria High. Grade point average, 3.9. Allergies, nuts.

My eyes continue to skim over my own statistics, down to the more nitty-gritty. Mental health.

Her brother Finn was found to be schizoaffective when they were five, diagnosed by American doctors and treated with Lithium and Haldol, with the occasional Xanax for panic attacks. Symptoms of his disease are hallucinations, delusions, mood swings, mania/depressions.

Calla on the other hand…

"What are you doing in here?"

I recognize Sabine's voice immediately from her stance in the doorway, and I fluidly close the file and slide it back in the drawer in one motion.

"Uh…" my heart pounds. "I'm hunting for something."

Sabine doesn't move, but her dark eyes gleam in the night.

"What are you searching for, child?"

I watch her face, waiting for her to flip on the light, for her to pick up her phone and call Eleanor, waiting for her to do something. But she doesn't. She lingers in the doorway, waiting for me to answer.

"Explanations," I offer unapologetically, not moving from where I stand.

Sabine enters the room soundlessly, her tiny body moving across the room.

"Answers that are not freely given aren't really answers at all," she tells me, each word a mystery.

I take a step, then another, then pause.

"Do you know the answers, Sabine?"

Sabine cocks her head, her white hair glowing in the night. "I know more than many, but my answers aren't ones you would like," she finally says.

"I was afraid of that," I sigh. "Do you know what time Dare got home tonight?"

Sabine looks at me curiously. "I wasn't paying close attention. He went into town to buy flowers for his mother. I'm sure he spent time in the crypts tonight. He usually does, child. You aren't the only one who suffered a loss, you know."

I know.

"Is there something I should know about his mother?" I whisper, staring at the old lady, imploring her. "I feel like there is."

Sabine stops moving, her wrinkled hand on the door. "Use the sense God gave you. You have instincts for a reason, we all do. Listen to them. And don't get caught in Eleanor's study again."

With that, the old woman is gone and I'm left alone in the chilling room. The very air in here feels like Eleanor, heavy, stern, smelling like orchids. It's cloying and unpleasant, much like Eleanor herself.

I rush to leave. When I'm all the way down the hall, I have the overwhelming need to turn around, and when I do, I almost expect Eleanor to be standing there, to be watching me.

But of course no one is there.

Whitley is getting to me.

I hurry toward my room, but once I reach it, I hear voices coming from within.

Finn's voice.

My imagination has unleashed itself, and I dash inside my room to find my brother thrashing about, muttering words I can't understand.

He looks up at me, his eyes wild and blue, and I sink down next to him.

"Finn. Take a breath. You can breathe, you're fine. I'm fine. You're fine. It's all going to be ok."

"No," he mutters. "No, no, no."

"Come here," I attempt to persuade him. "You're fine. Finn, you're fine."

Finn sits up, and his eyes are glazed, a crazy look in them. He's not in reality right now, that much is apparent.

"One for one for one," he mutters, turning to stare out the window. "Do you hear that, Cal? That's them. One for one. I'm one, you're one, he's one."

"Who's *he*, Finn?" I ask, humoring him.

"Him," Finn says impatiently. "The one with the black eyes, Cal. You know who. One for one for one. The die has been cast. It's cast, it's cast."

"You're fine, Finn," I tell him softly. "You're fine. I'm here."

You're dead, and I'm imagining you.

I can control my thoughts.

But I can't.

Because I will Finn away, and

He's still here thrashing on the floor.

He mutters for a while longer and then curls up, his head in my lap. I stroke his back and his shoulders, attempting to calm him. It's odd how easily I can remember what his arms feel like, how easily I can envision him even now.

"His eyes are black, Cal. His eyes are black."

Finn lets his face roll to the side, and his hands clench in front, so tight that his knuckles turn white.

"He's dangerous, Cal. His eyes are black. Black, black, black."

He's staring and I follow his gaze, and I'm startled to find Dare standing at our door, watching us.

Watching *me,* because Finn isn't actually here.

He's dangerous, Cal.

Dare's eyes are so dark that in the right light, they do look black.

"I'm sorry," he apologizes, backing away. "Is everything all right? Do you need anything?"

I shake my head and he goes away and I'm left reeling.

His eyes are black, Cal. He's dangerous.

I suppose he is.

That's why I've felt so uneasy, like he's hiding something.

He's dangerous.

But why?

All I know is, when he leaned against my doorway, one thing popped into my head.

He's a weapon, armed for obliteration.

And if I'm not careful, the obliteration will be my own.

Chapter Thirteen

I watch Finn walk peacefully around the pond that borders the back of the gardens, and I ponder how completely different he is today than he was last night.

Last night, he'd been desperate, out of his head.

Today, he's peaceful and calm.

Like magic.

You'd think that since I'm imagining him, I could control his actions, but apparently, like always, he does what he wants.

"It's ok to pretend your brother is still here."

Surprised, I turn to find Sabine approaching from behind. Somehow, she always seems to move silently through the rooms of Whitley, and appears when I least expect her.

"How did you know?" I ask, my cheeks flushing with embarrassment. Only a crazy person would do something like this, yet Sabine isn't acting like I'm crazy. She's calm, she's quiet, she's respectful.

"As long as you know the difference between reality and your thoughts, all is well," she tells me easily, as though she's a guest at the White Rabbit's tea table.

I swallow hard because I'm the rabbit.

"He's at peace now, you know," Sabine tells me, sitting down next to me. "Demons chased that boy. They don't now."

I suck in a breath, glancing at the old woman. "How did you know that?"

She shrugs. "I know things."

I swallow hard. I sense she knows *things*. So many things are in her eyes, so many truths. It scares me a little.

"He first started seeing things when we were in kindergarten," I tell her quietly, my memories bitter in my mouth. "He saw demons. He's seen them for years. He's medicated now. I mean, before he died. Sometimes, he forgot to take them…"

Sabine nods and I know she understands. Somehow.

"It's good for you to be here," she tells me seriously. "Away from death. Your mother would think so, too."

I look at her quickly. "You think so?"

"Yes," Sabine answers. "I knew her well. She'd want you to focus on yourself here without inhaling death in the air. It'd be good for anyone. We absorb the energy that's around us, you know. Energy never goes away. It just goes from thing to thing to thing."

That actually makes sense. In fact, it's a scientific fact. The law of conservation of energy states that energy cannot be created or destroyed, it can only change form. Here outside of the house, the energy is quiet and peaceful.

I definitely should absorb some of that.

"Where do you think my brother is?" I ask hesitantly. "If energy can't be destroyed, I mean."

Sabine crosses her arms. "You carry him with you," she says confidently.

I fiddle with my fingers. "I know. I...yes. But where do you think he *actually* is?"

Sabine looks away, far off into the distance, and when she answers, it's slow and sure.

"I have many beliefs, Calla. And I'm not sure you want to hear them all. Just know that you're not alone. You're never alone."

I'm not sure if that's comforting, actually.

But she's already changing the subject.

"I'm an expert in herbs, Miss Price. I learned from my mother, who learned from her mother, who learned from hers and so on. I can give you a tea to help with your sleep. I wish I would've known your brother. I have a feeling I could've helped him, too."

I immediately shake my head. "I don't think so. Your herbs might've interacted with his meds. He took some pretty strong medication. He had some pretty crazy days."

But then again, I should talk.

"You never know," Sabine tells me. "But know this. You shouldn't dismiss your brother as 'crazy'. People like him, people who suffer from that type of affliction, their minds are open; they don't see things for what they were supposed to be, they see things for what they *are*."

I'm confused now, and a little bemused. "So you're saying that the demons my brother saw were real?"

Even I can hear the humor and condescension in my voice, and I try to check it. At the very least, Sabine is my elder and I need to respect that. She shrugs.

"Perhaps. Who are we to say?"

"People like Finn are more inclined to trust their intuitions," Sabine continues. "They're very intuitive. You should take a page from that book."

My head snaps around and she chuckles. "No offense intended, of course."

"Of course," I murmur.

For some reason, as the breeze blows across the lawns, my attention turns to the horizon, where I know a lonely mausoleum sits by itself, forgotten by the people within Whitley.

"How did my grandfather die?" I ask her bluntly, changing the subject as I think of the lonely crypt. Sabine doesn't flinch.

"He had a car accident in the rain."

"And my uncle?"

She stares at me, her dark gaze unwavering. "He also had a car accident."

"In the rain?"

"Isn't it always raining here?" Sabine answers a question with a question. I sigh.

"That's quite a coincidence. Father and son both killed in car accidents."

Sabine shrugs again, unconcerned with it.

"The universe has a funny way of working, Miss Price."

"What do you mean by that?"

The old lady stares into the horizon, seeing things that I can't.

"The universe takes care of iniquities, of people who have been wronged, of injustices that the world can't right. That's all I meant."

I exhale, my breath slightly shaky. "That's all? That's quite a belief. It seems like you're saying that people can be cursed by the universe."

"That's exactly what I'm saying," she acknowledges. "It's true. I'm sorry if you're scared by that."

"I'm not scared," I admit. "I just don't think I subscribe to that particular belief system."

Sabine smiles now, and the only thing that I'm scared of is her grotesque smile. It's not pleasant.

"Surely you've noticed unfair things," she points out. "Growing up the way you did. I'm sure you've seen deaths that weren't fair. Stillborns, children, young mothers, young fathers... didn't you wonder what happened to make them occur?"

I stare at her dumbfounded. "Life isn't fair, Sabine," I tell her firmly. "That's all there is to it. People don't always deserve what happens to them. Not by a long shot."

I think about my brother, and the demons that chase him. *"Not by a long shot."*

Sabine is unfazed. "There are times we pay for sins that are not our own," she maintains. "It is the way the universe has always been."

I reflect on that for a minute, of my gentle father and my kind mother. There is no way either of them could've ever committed a sin bad enough for Finn to have paid for it. I shake my head finally, to signal my disbelief. Sabine smiles slightly.

"Take Adair for example," she instructs me. "That boy has never done anything wrong. Yet his parents were all killed. His father died from cancer, then his mother re-married Dickie Savage. Dickie wasn't a good man, and Dare's childhood wasn't either. Dickie died, then Olivia, and Dare was left all alone. Do you think he deserved any of that?"

I shake my head slowly. "I don't know. I don't know what he deserves."

"Use your intuition, Calla," Sabine instructs, and I can't help but remember the vulnerability on Dare's face the night I found him playing the piano in the moonlight. I can't help but picture the face *that I love.*

"No," I admit. "I don't think he deserved those things." *How could anyone deserve those things?*

"Sometimes the son must pay for the father's sins. Or the mother's," Sabine adds.

That thought gives me pause, the injustice of it. "That hardly seems fair," I tell her, picking a flower from the bed beside me.

"Life isn't fair," Sabine answers. "That's the first hard lesson." She crushes the flower she's holding in her gnarled hand, then drops the tangled petals on the ground at my feet. "Don't forget it."

She walks away as Finn approaches me, interest in his imaginary eyes.

"What was she saying to you?" he asks as he takes her vacated seat. I shake my head.

"Nothing important," I lie. "She's a strange one, Finn. I don't know what to think about her."

"Me either," he answers. "She kind of scares me a little."

This, coming from the boy who sees demons.

"Mom trusted her," he offers. "Maybe you should, too."

I nod silently. Maybe.

"She said you have good intuition," I tell him. "So what does your gut say about her?"

He grins at me. "Oh, so she sees the wisdom of my ways?" He closes his eyes and pretends to think, his brow wrinkled. "I think... she's odd. And I withhold the right to reserve judgment until later."

"Cop out," I accuse him.

He grins wider. "It's my right. I'm the wise one, apparently."

I roll my eyes. "Lord help us."

We make our way inside for a quiet lunch, for which neither Eleanor nor Dare join us. The dining room is utterly silent, but for my chewing sounds and china and silver scraping.

"Do you think it's weird that we never see Eleanor?" I ask Finn when we're finished.

He shrugs. "I don't care one way or the other. To be honest, I'm sort of glad I'm not there with you. I don't want to deal with Eleanor."

"Gee, thanks."

But I get it.

I don't blame him.

This time, I don't even think it's a twin thing. I'm sure everyone must feel the same way about Eleanor.

Before bed, I try to call dad, and my call can't be completed. I apparently have no signal.

"Maybe I can go into town tomorrow and try," I mention as I grab my pajamas to change in the bathroom.

Finn stares at me drolly. "Or you could just call him on the house phone."

I scrunch up my face. "I don't know why, but I feel weird about it. Like someone is listening. Always."

"Everyone is wrong," he announces suddenly. "You're the crazy one, Cal. Not me. Why would people be listening to your phone calls?"

"I don't know," I have to admit. "I just feel like they are. I can't help how I feel."

"No, you can't. But you can help how you process those feelings," he tells me helpfully. "Trust me, you don't want to be crazy, Calla."

Without another word, I leave to put my pajamas on. When I come back out, he's already curled up on one side of my large bed. It's unspoken now that he'll stay with me while I sleep. He knows I don't like being here alone. This huge place makes me feel small.

Even though my father hasn't answered any of my letters yet, I write him again.

I write until I can't hold my eyes open anymore, but even though I'm exhausted, my sleep isn't restful.

Dreams about Finn consume me. His face, his skinny arms and legs as he runs from something. With horror, I realize that he's running from *me*.

"You don't understand," he shouts over his shoulder, running toward cliffs. Are those the cliffs back home?

"What don't I understand?" I yell back, the rain pelting my face, drenching my clothes.

"What it's like to be me!" his voice is hoarse, and it cracks under his shriek. He skids down the mountain, and suddenly Dare is with him, and they're

running together, a unified front, both teaming up against me.

"Stay back!" Dare shouts to me. "You're only making it worse."

"Making what worse?"

"Everything," he tells me, his handsome face earnest. "Just stay away. It's the best thing you can do. You'll be our downfall."

"The end is the beginning, Calla," Finn adds. "Please. GO. Go back, go back."

"Go back where?" I scream. "Home? I want to, but I can't. Not without you, Finn."

Is this a dream?

The colors are real, Finn's voice is loud, and Dare's face is beautiful.

"The beginning," Finn yells. "The end is the beginning. Don't you understand?"

I sit straight up in bed, gasping, my hands clenched around the sheets.

Finn is dead. He's not on the cliffs and neither am I.

We're safe.

Aren't we?

I'm not so sure anymore. An overwhelming feeling of unrest surrounds me, and sleep is impossible for the rest of the night.

***

When I go for my morning walk, I bump into Sabine yet again. It feels like she's always near.

"Have you found the secret garden yet?" she asks.

This grabs my attention. "Secret garden?"

She smiles. "It's at the end of the path that leads by the stables, a few acres from the house. Grab a bicycle and find it. It's enclosed by a stone fence, and you'll feel alone there, I promise. It's hidden from the house."

It sounds like something out of a storybook, and I do exactly what she says. I grab a bicycle from the stable and follow the trail.

It ends exactly as she described, with a garden encircled by a stone fence, too tall to see over. It has a wooden gate and I open it without hesitation, the hinges squeaking.

Once I'm inside, I'm awestruck, and I stand frozen, staring around.

The garden is at once natural and cultured, landscaped and overgrown. Filled with vibrant colors and smells, it's a jewel hidden behind walls, absolutely gorgeous.

"What the…" I breathe. I can't imagine who takes care of it. Who manages to make it seem so natural, yet still so perfect?

There's an enclosed gazebo with stone pillars, and several large stone angels. They seem to guard the perimeter, watching with sightless eyes. They put me a bit on edge, but that might be due to the fact that they're over nine feet tall.

Benches are strewn here and there, and tiny little ponds. Birds chirp, crickets cheep, and the sounds of water lull me into calm. It's perfection.

"I see you've found my sanctuary."

The voice is deep, and before I even turn around, I know who it is.

Dare.

"This is yours?" I ask, well aware that it existed long before he was born. It was probably created for my mother.

"It is now," he shrugs. "I'm the only one who comes here. Until today, that is."

"You don't seem like a garden kind of guy," I observe, staring at his tailored slacks and v-necked shirt. The corner of his mouth tilts up and the breeze ruffles his dark hair.

"Maybe not. But I'm a private kind of guy. And this place is that. Plus, it's the only place on this entire property that doesn't feel creepy."

I can't argue that. It feels like the only bit of sunlight in a perpetually cloudy day. And while I came here looking for solitude, I have to be honest and admit to myself that I don't mind sharing it with Dare. Even though I'm supposed to be pushing him away.

"Do you have a job?" I ask him suddenly, as the idea that he's hanging out in a garden at ten in the morning occurs to me. He grins now, a full-on smile that spreads across his face. It's as bright as the sun and I revel in it.

"Depends on your definition. Don't you know that working is beneath the Savages?"

"But you're not a Savage," I point out hesitantly. Is he sensitive about that?

He grins again, authentic and nonplussed. "No, I'm not. But you are. You'll have to get used to simply having money, and pretending to do worthwhile things."

"I want to *do* worthwhile things, not just pretend," I tell him stoutly.

He looks down at me before sliding gracefully onto a bench.

"I believe you," he offers.

I feel awkward as I stand, while he so casually sits. My presence must not affect him like his does me.

"What do you do all day here?" I ask, fidgety in the silence. He glances up at me.

"I fill my time with this or that. It's been a long time since I was here without you. To tell you the truth, with my old ways behind me, I'm at a loss."

"Your old ways?"

His mouth twitches. "In the old days, someone wouldn't ask me *what* I do all day, they'd ask me *who.*"

Lord have mercy.

"I didn't need to know that." In fact, the knowledge makes me a bit queasy.

His lip twitches again. "You said you didn't want secrets. I figure some normal conversation will do you good. I didn't used to be nice. But then *you* happened."

"And now?"

"I'm still not nice, but I *am* with you."

"I miss you," I whisper bluntly, because oh my God, I do. I miss everything about him. I miss his smell, I miss his arms, I miss the LIVE FREE tattooed on his back. I miss everything about him.

With one deft movement, he dips his head and before I even know it, his mouth is on mine. His lips are firm yet soft, and he tastes like mint. I exhale into his mouth, almost a sigh, and he grips my back.

And then very abruptly, he releases me.

"I miss you, too."

I inhale a shaky breath, fighting the urge to lift my fingers to my mouth, to feel where his lips had just been.

"Why did you do that?" I whisper, not complaining, but just so, so confused.

There's actually confusion in his eyes, too.

"Because no matter what, I refuse to let you go."

And then he leaves me standing alone in the garden.

Chapter Fourteen

I stay in the garden alone for the longest time.

In fact, the afternoon has begun the slow turn into evening, the horizon red and orange and amber, before I finally head back to the house, my head somewhat clear and my heart light.

My fingers trail over my lips, the memory of Dare's kiss still fresh.

The garden has washed away the heavy feeling that I normally carry, the foreboding and the fear. For right now, in this moment, when I think of Dare, all I think of is *want*.

I want him.

Regardless of the consequences.

Whatever those consequences might be.

The feeling is short-lived however.

The strange man steps out ahead of me on the path, still wearing gray pants and a hoodie, his hood still pulled up tightly around his face.

My breath flutters and I pause on the stones, part of me wanting to run, and part of me wanting to chase him.

I must be crazy because I'm not afraid, even though I'm a woman out walking alone and he clearly shouldn't be here.

Something about him seems lonely and sad,

And I can relate to that.

Is he a groundskeeper son, maybe?

He lingers on the path, waiting, and I sense that he wants me to follow.

"Who are you?" I call, taking one step.

He turns his face, slow...slow...slow.... and just when I think I'll see it, I'll see his face, he stops. His identity is just out of sight, just like he wants it to be.

He wants to play a game.

He turns, hurrying down the path.

But when I fall behind, he waits.

He wants me to follow him.

He takes a step, and so do I. Then we take another, then another.

I'm with a magnificent curiosity, bigger than I've ever felt, and I'm compelled to follow him even against my logical judgment, to play this game and see where it leads me.

Mist floats across the path, hiding his legs, but then he's inside the house, disappearing into hallways. I call out to him to stop, but he doesn't.

He turns down a hallway.

I follow.

He turns again, then again.

Finally, he stands in front of Sabine's bedroom door. He faces it, his forehead almost resting on the wood.

And then just as I reach him, he's gone.

I stand bewildered and confused, alone in front of Sabine's door.

The man was as real as I am, but yet he's just simply not here.

I'm crazycrazycrazy.

I take a deep breath, because one thing is sure in my crazy mind. Real or not real, he wanted to draw me to Sabine's door.

But why?

I knock, intent on finding out.

"Come in," the old lady calls.

I'm hesitant and scared. But my need to know outweighs my fear.

I enter her living quarters to find Sabine hunched over a table. She's concentrating, absorbed, something in her hands.

Sabine straightens now, and I see what she's holding.

Tarot cards.

"He won't hurt you," she says, unconcerned with my ire. "At least not right now. You'll have to trust me on that."

She saw him, too?

"I don't trust you," I reply. "I don't know you."

My mother trusted her. And that's the difference. She clucks, but doesn't answer.

"Who was he?" I ask, stepping further into the room.

Sabine shakes her head and returns her attention to the cards on the table. "Youth is wasted on the young," she declares before humming a tuneless song. She puts another card down, then another. "Use your instincts, girl. That's what God gave them to you for."

My instincts aren't talking at the moment *and why am I not afraid?*

It doesn't make any sense, and so I stare at the table.

The tarot cards are gold, glittering in the dying light from the window. The figures on the cards are drawn in rich colors, dark reds and blues and greens. They look so mystic, so powerful and forbidden. In spite of everything, I'm intrigued.

The card she's holding is a knight, and he appears to be preparing to swallow a handful of swords. Sabine notices my gaze.

"The Four of Swords," she tells me without looking up. "He signifies rest after a period of struggle or stress or pain."

She lays another card down, half obscuring the Four of Swords. "This is the Six of Swords," she explains, still not looking at me. "He symbolizes moving out of stormy waters into calmer ones. If someone has experienced hard times, this card means that things will very shortly be looking up for them, that harmony will soon be restored."

"Who's cards are you reading?" I ask her, trying not to sound too interested. "Your own?"

She shakes her head once. "Your brother's."

I suck in a breath. "Finn's?"

She nods without answering, examining the array of cards in front of her.

"He's dead. What's the point?"

She ignores me, still examining the cards as if I hadn't spoken.

I wait patiently, counting my breaths, until she finally looks up.

"Page of Cups. Water is your brother's element. He's got the vulnerability of a child, and he trusts like a child, as well. He's good-hearted, thoughtful, kind. He's also artistic and creative. He's very intuitive, but criticism crushes him. He doesn't have many friends, because he's not understood well by others. Does this sound like him?"

Only completely.

I nod. "Yeah. A bit." Sabine nods knowingly, and lays one last card down. She stares at it, then smiles.

"These are good," she tells me, seemingly satisfied. "I like these cards for your brother."

"But...he's dead," I tell her again, so so so confused. "He's gone."

"Lord, child," Sabine exclaims, shaking her old head. "Haven't we already discussed this? Energy is never really gone."

"The energy here at Whitley scares me," I tell her hesitantly. "It's dark and there's something here that I …"

Sabine looks up, her eyes thoughtful. "That you what?"

I look away. "I don't know. I feel unnerved here. Unsettled."

"You were right to come here," she finally answers. "It was the only way."

"The only way for what?"

I think I'm afraid to know the answer.

"You'll have to answer that," Sabine says sagely. "You're the one who will know."

I once again feel like I've been dropped in a rabbit hole, and I'm not sure who is the crazy one, Sabine or me.

Right now, though, my money is on Sabine.

"Sit," she tells me. "I'm going to read your cards."

"That's not necessary," I tell her, backing away. "Really."

She stares at me wordlessly, until I finally sigh and sink to a seat in a chair in front of her. It might be a load of crap, but it won't hurt anything.

Probably.

She shuffles the cards, then offers them to me. "Draw one."

I do, and she splits the deck where I touched.

One by one, she methodically lays the cards out in a cross shape.

"The Three of Swords," she murmurs. "It means you're separated from someone you love."

"My mom and Finn," I nod. She clucks.

"Yes. But you're separated from someone else you love, and it's a self-imposed separation. You didn't have to do it, but you did anyway. Curious."

Dare. His loss is just as painful.

She sticks her nose back in the cards.

"The Six of Wands." She glances up. "The fruits of your labor will pay off somehow. Your efforts will be successful."

"My efforts with what?"

She doesn't answer. She's already on to the next card.

"Hmm, interesting." She peers at the card in her hand, then glances up at me. "The Nine of Cups. It's sometimes referred to as the Wish card. Something you desire will bring you fulfillment."

"What do I desire?" I ask quietly. There's one thing I desire more than anything, for Finn to still be alive. And her freaking cards can't help with that.

A small smile dances across her lips.

"The cards don't tell me that. That is for you to know."

She picks up the next card.

"Ah, this one I would expect. The High Priestess. It symbolizes a duality of forces, the moon and stars. The High Priestess can access the psyche and the conscious, she can defy natural laws. But she also represents mystery and secrets."

"And what does that mean in English?" I ask dumbly.

"It means that you and Finn are halves of a whole. It also means that you don't know yourself yet, that you have many parts. The rest you must discover on your own."

I sigh.

I feel her gaze on me. "This one is interesting. The Lovers."

My head snaps up. "And that one means?"

Sabine looks back at the table. "It's self-explanatory."

Heat flushes my cheeks and I drum my hand against my leg. "That one must be a mistake."

"I don't make mistakes," she answers. "Use care with him, child. He's a good boy, but he'll be your ruin."

A flash of white hot fire rages through my gut in surprise. *He'll be my ruin?* How overly dramatic.

"I don't know who you're talking about," I deny, knowing full well who she means. She glances at me but for a second.

"Of course you do," she murmurs, but she doesn't say anything more because her attention is already on to the last card, and I only get a brief glance at a black skull before she very quickly flips it over.

"What was that?" I ask her curiously, but when I look at her expression, my stomach sinks. She looks positively stricken.

"It's nothing."

But it was very definitely *something*. The calm old woman is visibly shaken as she clears the cards and straightens them into a pile before putting them into a drawer.

"Come back next week," she suggests, her voice thin. "We'll read them again, child. Your tarot can change."

She sounds almost hopeful that it will.

Curious.

I leave Sabine to her room, and return to my own. Booting up my laptop, I can't help but do a search for tarot cards, so that I can find out what that last mysterious card meant.

It's only a matter of minutes before I find a similar card, a muted one with a dark skull in a black hood.

My heart quickens when I read the meaning.

It's the Death card.

Chapter Fifteen

There are a million clocks.

They cover all the walls and they're all tickingtickingtickingticking. I cover my ears and spin around, trying to get away from the ticking, trying to get away from all of the hands and minutes and seconds. But there aren't any doors. There's no way out. I don't know where I am, I only know that time is my enemy and the clocks are taunting me.

And then the clocks all turn into Dare's face. His smile is mocking me, and it is replicated a million times, and then there is his voice.

"Ask me, Calla Lily."

"I can't," I tell him. "I'm afraid."

"Don't be afraid of me," he answers. "I'm not the enemy. Time is."

"How do I get out?" I ask him, running from corner to corner.

"You're the only one who knows," he laughs. "What a silly question."

His laughter echoes and I startle awake.

It takes a minute to digest the dream, to come to terms with the fact that somehow, I was running from time.

How strange.

I can't go back to sleep, so I get dressed early and head to the dining room for breakfast. I expect to find it empty, so I'm unpleasantly surprised to find Eleanor already there.

She nods at me from the head of the table.

"Good morning," I tell her politely as I sit down.

"Is it?" she butters her croissant. I'm not surprised. Honestly, I would expect nothing less from Eleanor than her questioning how good a day will be before it even happens yet.

Before I can think of a good answer, Dare's voice fills the room.

"Good morning." He's got a baritone voice. I soak in it before I answer.

"Is it?"

I keep my voice droll, and Dare lifts an eyebrow as he sits across from me, in the place designated to him by Eleanor.

"Maybe it will be," he tells me. "Who knows?"

When I look at him now, I don't just see his chiseled jaw and handsome face. I see forbidden fruit. Someone I love, but someone I know I shouldn't...for reasons unknown.

That boy will be your ruin.

Lord have mercy. I take a bite of fruit, trying not to dwell on how he's been in my dreams lately. No one needs to know that but me.

He sips at coffee and Eleanor surprises us by addressing him.

"Have you been riding lately, Adair?"

Dare slowly turns his gaze toward her, very obviously reluctant.

"No, it's never been my cup of tea. Why?"

She stares down her nose disapprovingly at him.

"Your mother liked for you to ride."

Dare swallows his coffee and fixes his dark gaze grimly on the Savage matriarch.

"No, *Richard* liked for me to ride. My mother liked for us to please him."

He sounds disgusted by that, and by my uncle, too. It sends my thoughts spiraling. What exactly did Richard do to him?

"Well, either way. I know that Calla doesn't know how to ride, and I'd like for you to teach her. Educated young ladies should have that skill."

I practically swallow my grape whole.

"That won't be necessary," I choke. "I don't need to learn."

"Of course you do," Eleanor counters, and I can see that there will be no arguing.

She stands up and pushes her chair back, and the conversation is over. Clearly, I'll learn to ride and Finn won't, because that's how Eleanor wants it.

What Eleanor wants, Eleanor gets.

This is something I'm learning hard and fast.

Dare stares at me, humor on his lips and I can't decide what he finds funny. That I have to spend time with him, or that I'm controlled by Eleanor, just like everyone else.

"We might as well start this morning," he offers, taking a bite of toast and jam. He inadvertently smears just a bit on his lip, and the tiniest part of me wants to wipe it off for him, but I resist, of course, because he's an ass.

"Fine," I say instead, managing to sound bored and annoyed.

Because I am.

I won't let him affect me. I won't.

It's something I'm still repeating to myself as Dare helps me into the English saddle thirty minutes later. My butt is ungracefully shoved in his face and there's nothing ladylike about me as I kerplunk into the saddle. There's no saddle horn to grab so I'm unceremoniously awkward as I struggle to right myself.

"The most important thing is to have balance," Dare eyes me doubtfully as I sprawl on top of the massive animal. "Lightly squeeze the horse with your thighs. Pretend it's me, Cal."

Heat flares through me and I look away, trying not to remember what it felt like to be with him, to have him hover above me in the night.

My stomach flutters and Dare's lip twitches, like he knows exactly what I'm thinking.

"Keep the reins even, not too slack," he continues. "Sit upright. Don't be nervous, or your horse will feel it. Your horse's name is Jupiter's Many Moons. We call him Jupiter for obvious reasons. He's tame and he won't unseat you. Questions?"

Dare doesn't wait, he digs his heels into his horse's sides and they take off at a brisk trot. Or what I think is called a trot.

And I'm left in my version of hell.

"I don't like riding much!" I call to him, but he doesn't answer. I have a view of his backside, and even though I'm annoyed, I have to marvel at how at home he seems in the saddle. He doesn't look like a cowboy. He looks like a refined gentleman, like you could stick a polo stick in his hands and he'd be perfectly at home.

He pauses his horse with a low *whoa* and turns to me.

"To stop, pull back on the reins and say whoa."

"Got it."

I grip the reins tight. "Do you ever just wear t-shirts here, or do you always dress up?" Because he's wearing a collared polo right now. And while he does look fantastic, I just wonder if he ever feels at home here, the way he seemed to back in Astoria.

He smirks. "Eleanor would say that's beneath us."

"But you don't care what Eleanor thinks," I point out. "That much is obvious."

"I'm here right now, aren't I?" His dark eyebrow is raised, and even though I can't argue, I wish I could. A part of me, deep down, wishes that he were here because he wanted to be.

"You might not like riding, but you're good at it."

Without realizing it, I leave myself wide open and Dare grins.

"You know I'm good at riding everything."

He says *everything* in the most provocative way I've ever heard and he does it on purpose, to get a reaction from me. I swallow hard.

"I'm sure you've had no complaints," is all I say and he glances at me.

"About last night..." he begins and I roll my eyes.

"I'm sure you have to start many conversations with those words," I interrupt.

He smirks again.

"Perhaps. But seriously, I do apologize. That wasn't in good form. You weren't ready to kiss me again, and I shouldn't have forced it."

What a British thing to say. Something about it, and his accent, sends my heart into somersaults.

"I liked it," I admit quietly, and the words are out before I can take them back or hide them.

He's clearly pleased by my answer, so I add, "But it doesn't change anything. I still need space."

Even though I want you more than ever.

His face clouds over and we fall silent. Finally, I can't take it anymore and ask the first thing I can think of.

"Do you like it here?" I ask as we guide our horses onto the quiet lane outside of the driveway. Their hooves make clipped sounds on the cobbles, and I decide that I'm quite good at this.

"No," his answer is immediate and short. "You?"

"No," I sigh.

"You should get used to it. It's where you're from," is all he offers.

I sigh again.

"You don't like riding, do you?" he asks now, more polite than interested.

I shake my head. "No. I feel bad for the horse. Why should he have to carry me around?"

Dare chuckles, then leans forward, digging his heels into his horse. "You can't weigh more than eight and a half stones. He doesn't even notice you, I'm sure. But follow me."

He trots ahead, then begins a slow canter. My horse does the same, and I hold on for dear life, my heart racing from the thrill of it. Dare leads me back to the stables.

"We'll ride something a bit more fun."

I stare at him in confusion as we dismount and hand the reins to the groom.

My eyes widen as I follow Dare to the garage, and we stop in front of a sleek black motorcycle. I should've known he'd have a bike here.

But the English countryside is wet and the roads are curvy, and I'm hesitant.

"Do you know how many people have passed through my dad's funeral home because of motorcycle accidents?"

And I'd have to wrap my body around yours, holding you tight.

I can't.

I can't.

I turn around and start to walk away, but Dare grabs my elbow.

"Come on, Calla. You've got to live a little bit."

"That's exactly what I'm trying to do," I tell him as I turn back around. "I won't live long on the back of that thing."

He grins his freaking *dare me* grin, though, and I know that I'm a goner. It sets a fire in my belly because it's real. It's like I can see a tiny bit of his old self shining through, and I can't resist that. He sees it on my face and grins even wider.

"You need a helmet. There's an extra in that cabinet."

He points to the wall, and I retrieve the helmet, and I put it on with shaking fingers.

We're roaring down the road a few minutes later, and I have my arms wrapped around Dare's strong body.

Within seconds, I've decided that this is Heaven.

I'd forgotten how good this feels.

I rest my cheek against his shoulder, and we blow through the gates of Whitley.

The wind hits my cheeks, the seat vibrates beneath me, and Dare's back flexes as he balances the bike. I've never felt so exhilarated in all my life.

The countryside around us is beautiful, dotted with flowers amid all the green, and I watch it blur as we ride faster and faster. I don't even feel afraid, and I know I can attribute that sense of well-being to Dare. He's an expert at riding this thing, and I'm safe behind him, even on the wet and winding roads.

We don't go far though, before he slows the bike, and we pull onto a gravel road leading to a pond. It's remote, it's quiet, and I have no idea what we're doing.

So I ask.

Dare offers his hand and helps me off the bike.

"You're going to live."

I arch an eyebrow hesitantly.

"I'm living right now," I tell him.

He shakes his head. "Not really. Come on."

For a reason I can't explain, I willingly follow him, regardless of my hesitancy, and the way my cautious side is throwing up red flags left and right.

Dare stops on the edge of the pond, and unbuttons his pants.

I freeze in place as his trousers pool around his feet and he steps out of them. His muscles form V-shaped ribbons that disappear into his underwear. I know where they lead. I look away, my cheeks flushed.

He immediately strips off his shirt, tosses it onto the bank, then stands in front of me in black boxer-briefs.

My heart ricochets against my ribcage and I can't help but stare.

His abs form individual striations, ripped and strong. His biceps bulge and then blend into the leanness of his arm, and I have the sudden urge to trace all of it with my fingers, like I have a hundred times before, so I ball my hands into fists.

"What are you doing?" I struggle with words, but finally manage.

"Swimming."

He turns and heads into the water without flinching from its cold temperature. I suck in a breath because he's got that freaking tattoo on his back, spanning across his shoulder-blades. Black words that read: LIVE FREE.

I'm a goner. A freaking goner.

"There's a pool at Whitley," I call out to him. "And I think it's heated."

Dare laughs and dives under the water, coming right back up, shaking droplets out of his hair.

"It's not as fun."

"Why is this fun?" I have to ask. Because the water is cold, there's bugs, there's mud.

Dare stares at me drolly. "Because we're trespassing. This isn't our property."

This surprises me and gives me pause.

"The owners don't know you're here?"

"Nope," Dare answers, unconcerned, back-pedaling away from me, without taking his eyes off my face. "Does that scare you, my little rule-follower?"

His little rule-follower.

"Again, I ask you," my voice wavers a bit. "Why are you suddenly being so nice?"

He shrugs, his shoulder bare and glinting in the light. "Because you're mine, Calla. You just need to remember it. Now come swimming."

"I don't have a suit."

"You don't need one."

I counter and he parries.

My whole life, I've been a rule-follower. I've done what is expected, I've taken care of my brother. Maybe… just maybe….

Before I can change my mind, I'm pulling my shirt over my head and shoving my pants down. Without looking at Dare, and with my face exploding into tomato red flame, I follow him into the water in my bra and panties.

It's cold enough to take my breath away, or that might just be my exhilaration at breaking the rules. I can't be sure.

"Have you come here before?" I suck in a breath around chattering teeth as I paddle in Dare's direction.

He nods. "Plenty of times." I don't want to ask who else he's brought with him.

"And the owners have never caught you?"

He grins. "Oh, they've caught me. But I can't be tamed."

I giggle at that, at the matter-of-fact way he said it.

I start to grow accustomed to the cold temperature and my teeth stop chattering.

Dare swims back and forth a few times, then treads water while he observes me. Oddly enough, and probably because the water keeps my body hidden, I don't feel self conscious.

"I think you're a closet rebel," Dare announces. I have to laugh at that.

"Not hardly," I admit. "I'm terrified right now that the owners of this property are going to find us and call the police."

"First, we call them coppers here," Dare explains with a snicker. "And second, you don't seem to understand the power of your name yet. Savages can do anything they like around here."

"But you don't consider yourself a Savage," I remind him as I tread water. Something akin to warmth floods his eyes, and his mouth tilts up in the crooked grin that I am beginning to love. When he's not smiling, I wait for it to appear, like an addict waiting for a fix.

"I fall under the same umbrella, though," he tells me. "At least, for outsiders looking in."

"Did you know that you speak in riddles?" I ask him in annoyance. He dives under water without answering, and within two seconds, he's grabbed my ankle, pulling me under with him.

I struggle and twist, but he pulls me down, down, down, and then I'm against his wet hard body and suddenly, I don't want to struggle anymore. I don't want to push him away.

Not by a long shot.

His body is both strong and lean, cold and warm. It's very hard, and I'm held against it, reveling in it, soaking it in. He's angles and muscle, strength and grace.

He's moving against me, his hips, his hands.

His fingers glide fluidly against my skin, creating friction even beneath the water.

I'm on fire.

The warmth spreads from my arms to my legs to my belly.

It's a wild-fire, and suddenly I'm quite sure that he's the only thing that can put me out.

Together, we float to the surface, still intertwined. We break through the top and I suck in a breath and Dare is staring into my eyes.

There's tension here, but not the bad kind. It's the kind that ignites you, the kind that intoxicates you, the kind that once you taste it, you'll crave for the rest of your life.

I've forgotten that I was going to be careful, that I was going to reject him on every level.

All I can remember, all I can focus on, is how very *alive* Dare DuBray is making me feel in this moment, how alive he *always* makes me feel.

For a girl who has been surrounded by death her entire life, this is a very big deal.

"I'm a little afraid of you," I blurt honestly, and Dare still has his arms around me. Our treading water motions keep our legs rubbing together, the friction still there.

Hot,

Hot,

Hotter.

Dare smiles, but there is no humor in it.

"Good."

"Why?"

My honesty makes me seem innocent, but I don't know how to play games. I have no experience with the opposite sex at all.

"Because that makes you feel something."

But he's hesitant now and he looks away. There's something he wants to say, it's balanced on the tip of his tongue, but he swallows it.

"What is it?" I ask softly. "Just tell me."

He wants to, I can tell. His secrets are killing him. He just wants to be normal, he's just acting out a role.

I don't know why I feel like I know this. It's just there, suddenly resting on my heart.

"You don't have to be someone you're not," I murmur quietly. His dark eyes snap up to mine and he pulls his hands away. There's something in his eyes now, something guarded, and our easy afternoon has come to an end.

"What makes you think I am?" he snaps. "Pretending to be something I'm not, I mean."

I've somehow annoyed him, and I don't answer because I don't know what to say.

"I'm not being someone I'm not, Calla," he says coolly as he strides from the water. "I'm being who you need me to be. We've both experienced loss. You just can't handle yours."

I'm stunned because he's normally so patient, and I'm dripping wet.

"We don't have towels," is all he says when I follow him. My clothing soaks up the water and it is a very cold ride back home.

Dare doesn't say another word and I leave him in the garage.

I don't see him at dinner, and I don't see him the rest of the night.

But as I lay in bed around midnight, I see his car leave the garage.

I don't see him come home, and I'm awake for half the night waiting.

I have no idea where he goes when he slips away.

Somehow, I think he wants it that way.

There's a fork in the road and even though I see it, I can't avoid it.

One road goes left, one goes right, and neither of them ends well.

I feel it in my bones,

In my bones,

In my bones.

I sing a song of nonsense, and it sings back. The notes echo and twist in the air, and I swallow them whole.

"Come out," I call behind me, because I know they're there.

I can't see them, but they're always watching.

Eyes appear, blood red, and they blink once, twice, three times.

"I can see you," I announce and there's a growl and then I'm crushed beneath the dark, beneath the weight, beneath the oppression.

"You don't scare me," I lie.

There's savagery here, there's grace.

But above all, there's oblivion and no matter what I do, I will be sucked into it.

I know it.

I feel it.

I'm crazy.

VERUM

And it doesn't matter.
I'm the rabbitrabbitrabbit and I'll never be free.

Chapter Sixteen

For some reason that I can't explain, I'm holding my breath, waiting to see if Dare comes to dinner.

He does.

Dressed in black slacks, shiny black loafers and an oatmeal-colored soft shirt. He wordlessly moves across the room, sits in his seat, and places his napkin in his lap.

I look at my plate, remembering the way his hands touched me yesterday, the way I'd wanted it, the way I can't forget how he makes me feel.

My cheeks flush and I take a bite. They're both staring at me, or at least it seems that way.

"The fish is delicious," I finally offer, without looking up.

I think I hear Dare smile. My discomfort probably amuses him.

"Adair."

Eleanor's tone makes it sound like she just ate a persimmon.

"Yes?"

I look at Dare and it's easy to see that he can't hide his disdain.

"Play for us."

She commands him like a monkey, like he's expected to jump when she beckons, which of course he is. We all are.

Wordlessly leonine, he walks to the piano in the corner. Sitting at the bench, he gracefully does as he's told.

The song he plays is something sad and dark, which is perfect, because that's the mood I'm in. The notes brush my cheeks, play with my hair, and then fall limply onto the floor when he's done with them, after he strokes each of them from the keys.

I watch his hands and I can't help but remember yesterday, the way those same strong hands skimmed my wet body, tracing my curves. I can't help but remember how I'd let him touch me, how I'd folded into him.

I know I wouldn't have resisted if he wanted more.

But then he didn't.

I feel like I'm a lamb, and he's a wolf. But at the same time, I feel like he doesn't want to be. He's caged, when he should be wild, and I don't think he knows what to do about it.

The room is silent as we listen to his song, and I'm more emotionally charged by the minute. My past wells up in me, my present, my future. None of it looks good and then the music stops and my emotions pause.

Dare pushes the bench back, and he walks straight for me. My heart pounds as he bends, his lips close enough to graze my neck.

I remember those lips. The way they feel soft, yet firm. The way he tastes of spearmint.

"You smell like apples." His whisper is low. I close my eyes for a scant second, because an apple is what destroyed Eden.

I open my eyes.

"I'm sorry I was rude earlier. This is just so goddamned hard for me."

I know.

God, I know.

"Meet me in the garden tonight and I'll make it up to you. Midnight."

I glance up at him and I'm brave, but my bravery will get me eaten. Whether he wants to be or not, he's a wolf.

And I'm a lamb.

Dare walks away, because it doesn't matter to him what anyone thinks.

Dare does what he wants.

He lives free.

***

Midnight comes quickly.

I swing the gate open and tread inside among the night lilies, evening primrose and moonflowers. This garden is filled with things that are vibrant during the day and opulent at night. It is a small piece of paradise in the middle of a frightening place, and my mother had loved it. And so do I.

"Hey."

He's here already, and he lingers in the shadows, so at home in the night.

It reminds me of something my brother scribbled in his journal.

Nocte liber sum. By night I am free.

Am I free here with Dare?

"Hey," I answer, internally commending myself on my eloquence. "You're early."

"I wanted to be ready."

His voice is velvet, and it wraps around me like a blanket.

"What do you want with me, Dare?" I ask him honestly, because at the moment, I don't know. He's hot and cold, a distinct puzzle and I can't put him together.

"I can't do this anymore, Calla. It's too hard to watch you, to stay away from you...." his voice trails off. "We've been through so much already. Don't do this to us now."

"So again, I ask you, what do you want from me?" my words are simple, and I don't know what I'm doing.

Like always.

"That's a loaded question," he tells me as I approach and he watches my body as I move. I swallow hard because his expression is heavy and dark, and it's meant for me.

He's staring at me like he wants to eat me, and I am once again reminded that he's a wolf.

"So give me a loaded answer," I suggest, and my words surprise me *and* Dare.

What am I doing?

What am I doing?

His eyes widen, then narrow.

Dare practically growls as he yanks me to him, and he's hard against my body. I sigh into his mouth and he groans.

Sensations blur and conscious thought ceases.

Consequences be damned.

Sweet Lord.

Dare's tongue plunders my own and I've never felt so sexily invaded in my life. God, I've missed this. I've missed him.

So much,

So much,

So much.

It's like every nerve ending in my entire body has exploded, like I'm standing on fire, like I'm fire itself. I'm ore, I'm magma, I'm lava. I'm melted, I'm the sun.

He's ignited me.

His hands clutch me, big and strong and splayed against my back, and I somehow feel like I'm balanced in his hands, like he's holding me steady.

Maybe he is.

Maybe he always has.

My head falls back and he slides his lips along my neck, grazing the soft skin, inhaling my scent.

"You smell like apples," he tells me again, his voice husky in my ear. I feel urgent and rushed and desperate, yet his voice is even, controlled. I don't know how he's managing.

I pull back to ask, my hand on his rock hard chest, and suddenly the world spins.

Fragments, scents, sounds… so many things swirl together in my head and I'm not living in the present anymore.

I'm in the past,

And the past is a prison.

My eyes flutter closed because I can't take the overwhelming sensations, and even though I hear Dare's voice, asking me if I'm ok, I can't respond.

Because I see him.

Not in front of me in the moonlight, but in my head.

He's real, and he's familiar, and he's mine.

His face is twisted in pain, and he's trying to tell me something, but I don't want to listen. He's bloody, he's dark, he's broken.

He wasn't supposed to be there.

My memories are wrong.

But I can't find the right ones.

"Calla, are you ok?" he asks with bloody lips and his teeth are red.

I can't move,

I can't think.

He grabs me to him and screams,

And the scream builds into a roar,

And the roar is the ocean.

"Help!" Dare shouts, but I think it might've been me.

I close my heart, and he opens his lips, and words fall out, and I shake my head.

Because Finn is on the beach and he's dead.

And Dare has done something, something, something.

The fear grows and builds and takes me over, covering me up in shadows.

That boy will be your ruin, Sabine whispers. He'll breakyoubreakyoubreakyou.

In my head, blood spatters and someone screams and I yank away from Dare now, gasping for breath.

He's here,

and he's fine.

He's fine.

He stares at me, nervous, hesitant to approach.

"Are you all right, Calla?" his British words are clipped, and his eyes are concerned. He holds his hand out like he's soothing a disturbed filly, and I'm disturbed. That's the only thing to describe me.

Because none of that happened.

None of that is real.

Except for the fact that my brother is dead.

The nausea hits suddenly, in a frightening wave.

I whirl around so he can't see, and I retch into the bushes.

Humiliation swells in me, but not so much as the sickness.

Over and over, my stomach rebels, and I feel him behind me, trying to soothe me.

"Go," I tell him over my shoulder, utterly embarrassed.

"No," he answers firmly. "Maybe you have food poisoning. We should go see Sabine."

His answer for everything.

But somehow, I feel like she's causing this. I never felt this way until I met her. These things never happened to me before.

"No, not Sabine," I rasp, wiping my mouth and backing away. "I'm fine. I promise."

I'm lying. I'm not fine.

But he can't know that.

I spin around and flee, running for the house, running away from Dare. He lets me go, surprisingly. I glance over my shoulder when I'm bounding out the garden gates and he's standing limply, watching me with a strange expression.

I don't slow down until I reach the house.

I creep into my room and when I do, I imagine Finn waiting for me in the chair by the window, sitting in the dark.

Because that's what he would do if he were here.

He turns on the lamp.

If he were real.

"Where have you been?" he asks me quietly, judgment in his pale blue eyes.

"Out," I tell him. "I don't feel well."

"Did something happen?" he asks, cocking his head. "Did he do something to you?"

Annoyance fills me up. "Why would you assume he did something?" I demand, yanking my nightgown out of a dresser drawer. "You're imagining things. I just don't feel well."

He stares at me doubtfully. *"I'm* imagining things? Cal, this is getting dangerous. I don't know what you're up to, but it's not good."

I exhale a shaky breath, hating the way my lungs feel sick.

"I don't want you here tonight," I answer. And he's instantly gone, the chair vacant and dark, and I'm alone.

I turn my back, heading straight to the bathroom to change.

I don't know what's wrong with me.

All I know is, something is going on with me, something I don't understand. Something I don't want.

I run the water for a long time, splashing my face, cooling me down.

It doesn't help, and my dreams don't either.

I toss and turn in my bed, unable to wake even though I want to. My breathing quickens and I feel like I'm right on the cusp of…something.

Dare whispers. "Keep going. You're almost there. You can do this."

I don't know if I can.

I'm floating in an ocean of insanity. It's just ahead of me, so close I can touch it. But even though it shines and glimmers, it has glistening fangs and I know it will shred me.

"I'm scared," I whisper, gripping Dare's hands.

"You should be," he answers and his words impale me. "But it's ok. I'm here. You're not alone, Cal."

But I feel like it.

I'm alone.

I'm bobbing in a dark ocean and the lies surround me.

"Help!" I scream out, but no one is there, not even Dare.

"Finn!" I shout. "Please!"

No one answers.

No one comes.

I've been cast away, and I'll never be found.

Chapter Seventeen

"We must host an event at the end of the week for Savage Inc. I want you to be there. I think being among people might be good for you." Eleanor looks down her nose at me, and I squirm under her gaze. "That is all."

I nod and scramble to my feet, heading for the door.

"Oh, and one more thing."

We wait.

"Dress appropriately. The event will be formal."

Oh, perfect.

I hurry out and when I'm down the hall, Finn is waiting for me.

"I'm sorry about last night. It's not my business what you do."

But his eyes are still hurt and it makes me feel awful.

"No, I'm sorry," I tell him. "You were just being nice and I was being a bitch. I wasn't feeling well, but that's no excuse. I'm sorry, Finn."

He nods and all is forgiven, because he forgives me too easily. "Are you feeling better now?"

I nod. Because I am and I have no idea what was wrong with me last night.

"I was, until I heard we have to attend some formal party with the wicked witch."

"Ahem."

We whirl around to find Eleanor behind us. Her face is impassive despite the fact that she heard me call her a witch.

"I wanted to tell you that Jones will take you to London to be fitted for a gown. Who are you talking to, Calla?"

Her eyes meet mine, and for the briefest of moments, there's something almost human in hers. Something... concerned, maybe even hurt. But then she blinks and it's gone, and I must've imagined it.

"No one," I stammer. "Just myself."

She's unconvinced, I can tell. But she hesitates before walking away.

"You look very much like your mother, Calla."

She leaves now, her spine stiff and her posture completely rigid.

"Do you think Jones puts that rod up her ass every morning, or does she do it herself?" Finn snorts and I laugh at him, and the weird mood is broken.

I don't tell him that I have to stop thinking about him soon.

Thinking about him isn't helping me, it's pulling me into the past. It's something I know, even though I don't like it. I'm here at Whitley to get better, not regress.

But I'll address that a different day.

There's no reason to ruin today.

After breakfast, Jones takes me into London.

As we pull through the crowded city streets, I lean forward. "Do you have any suggestions on where to buy formal clothes, Jones?"

I'm thinking of my bank account nervously. The last I checked, it only had $237.26 in it.

Jones meets my gaze in the rearview mirror.

"I have orders from Mrs. Savage about where to take you, Miss Price. She's got it all arranged and has an account in the store."

Well, that's a relief.

I settle back into the seat.

"I've never had a tux before," Finn muses. Grief slams into me, because I know he hasn't. And now he'll never have the chance.

"You'd look amazing," I assure him. "Everyone looks stunning in a tuxedo."

The limo glides to a stop on the curb, and Jones is opening the door for me, his hand extended to help me out.

"Here you are," he says politely, motioning toward the door of a glitzy shop. "I'll be waiting for you."

I nod, and I'm greeted at the door by women in black uniform dresses and perfect red lipstick.

"Welcome, Miss Price," they tell me. "We've been expecting you."

It's a bit overwhelming as they usher us in and press warm drinks into our hands. One of them pulls me over to a tufted velvet sofa and settles me onto it.

"My name is Ginger," she tells me. "I'll bring out the gown Mrs. Savage ordered for you."

She turns on her high heel and disappears into a room, and I'm astounded. Eleanor ordered me a custom dress? When the heck had she done that? When we arrived?

Ginger returns after a mere moment with a demure pink silk gown draped in her hands.

She holds it up and I eye it.

It's long, with a sweetheart neckline and delicate hem, the palest of pinks.

I shrug. "Can I try it on?"

I'm not overly impressed and Ginger seems surprised.

"Of course, miss," she tells me, and leads me into a dressing room. She begins to undress me and I freeze.

"I can do this myself," I dismiss her.

"Are you sure?"

"I've been doing it all my life," I assure her. *Do rich people really let people dress and un-dress them?*

Holy cow. This isn't what I thought I was signing up for.

I pull the whisper-soft fabric on, and it drapes against me, fitting like only something expensive can. It's an innocent dress and it's beautiful, but to me, it washes my coloring out.

"I... um."

"Can I help?" Ginger calls over the door. I turn the handle and step out.

She eyes me.

"It fits you perfectly."

I can't argue with that. But it also does nothing for me. It's a dress for a twelve-year old, and it doesn't complement my coloring.

As I'm turning in the mirror, trying to like it, a swatch of crimson red catches my eye, and I gravitate it like the earth toward the sun.

Ginger trails behind, and I run the red satin beneath my fingers.

"This one," I say uncertainly. "It's beautiful. May I try it on?"

Ginger's hesitant. "This gown... it was made for someone else," she says slowly, but when I'm so obviously disappointed, she quickly adds, "But of course you can try it. We can always create another for Miss Aimes. I don't want to upset Mrs. Savage."

I don't correct her... I don't tell her that I would never say something bad about her to Eleanor, because she's so quick to try and keep me happy and I don't want to make her uncomfortable. It's clear that she's very intimidated by my grandmother.

She helps me out of the pale pink gown, and hangs it up while I put on the red.

As I turn around, she sucks in her breath. "Miss Price, you look stunning."

And I do. I examine myself in the mirror in surprise, because there is a stranger looking back. A woman with perfect curves and flushed cheeks, sparkling eyes and a stunning gown. The gown is strapless and although the top is just a smidgeon big, everywhere else hugs me just exactly right.

I am a woman in this dress.

If Dare could see me in this dress....

He has to see me in this dress.

"I wouldn't have thought the color would work with your hair," Ginger tells me. "But it's perfect."

"Can I have this one?" I ask hopefully, and Ginger nods.

"Of course. We'll create something new for Miss Aimes. This gown was clearly meant for you. We'll take in the bust about a half-inch, and it will fit you like a glove."

We pick out shoes and jewelry, and Finn is waiting for me in the car.

"I like being fancy," he decides, and he says it in a British accent. I giggle and start to reply, but I see something that gives me pause, a little café on a corner.

A dark-haired man sits in the café window.

Dare.

His face is intense, focused, and he's staring at the man across the table from him. He's not happy, far from it, in fact.

I can't see the other man, not clearly, even though I crane my neck. I can only partially see his face, the rest of him is hidden.

But he's firmly middle-aged, maybe fifty-something? Dark haired, and the one cheek that I can see looks flushed, a scarlet red flash of color.

Why are they upset?

Dare must feel me staring at him, and he turns, his dark eyes meeting mine. There is surprise in his, then dismay. I see it, I feel it, and then he looks away.

He's trying to pretend I didn't see him, and I wonder if I should do the same?

But he doesn't give me the chance.

After dinner, while Eleanor and Sabine are engaged in a quiet conversation in the library, Dare approaches me with his black slacks and his light cashmere sweater.

He's overwhelmingly handsome, and I struggle to pretend like he's not.

"Forget you saw me earlier," he tells me, and his voice is a little bit hard.

"What?" I ask in confusion, staring into his face, ignoring his chiseled jaw. He gazes down at me, so easily able to fluster me.

"You didn't see me in town." It's a directive and he means it.

I nod, not sure what else to do. Why is this so important?

"Ok," I agree. "I didn't see you. What were you doing that's such a secret?"

He glares at me now and I almost regret asking, but I don't. What *was* he doing?

"You can't know right now," he snaps, his lips lush and his tone ugly. "Trust me, you can't know yet."

"Why?"

He pauses, then looks at me, his eyes sincere and open and mine. "Because you would be lost."

As he walks away with the millions of hidden things in his eyes, I wonder if I already am.

***

I'm reading a book alone in the library when Sabine finds me, a cup of steaming hot chocolate in her hand. She sets it next to me, then sits in the adjacent chair.

"Dare is worried about you," she tells me.

"He told you that?" I ask doubtfully, because he was so annoyed with me earlier. She shakes her head.

"No. But I can see it."

I fight the urge to roll my eyes. "Don't worry about it. If he's truly concerned, he'll tell me."

Maybe.

But maybe I don't know anymore.

"I don't know that he would," Sabine answers. "You've pushed him away. He has no idea how to reach you now."

My chest hurts at that, because I know it's true.

"I don't want to talk about it,' I answer stiffly.

She nods and changes the subject.

"Your grandmother knows you changed your gown."

"Was it a secret?" I ask in surprise. "I didn't like the one she picked, it looked terrible on me. I chose a better color."

Sabine stares at me, humor in her old eyes. "She's not pleased," she tells me, but somehow, I feel like Sabine might be.

"You remind me of your mother," she adds.

"Everyone keeps saying that. Is it a bad thing?" I ask hesitantly.

She smiles. "No. It's a good thing. So curious and kind. I hope Whitley doesn't change you."

"It won't," I reply stoutly.

Sabine cocks her head, but doesn't answer. She stares out the window across the hall, and makes no motion to leave. I stare at her over the top of my book.

"Was there something else?"

I don't want to be rude, but I really want a minute alone, and something about this woman puts me on edge. She knows things better than I do... she knows Dare better, and she might even know *me* better. It's unsettling.

She turns her gaze to me, wise and old, and I fight the urge to flinch.

"We should read your cards again," she suggests. I do flinch now, and she chuckles.

"It's not a scary thing," she assures me. "My family has been doing it for hundreds of years. My mother, her mother, her mother. And so on."

"Only the women?" I ask, curious now. She nods.

"Only the women."

"Why?"

Why am I asking? This is clearly all lunacy.

She doesn't bother answering.

"Have you been feeling all right?" she asks instead. I hesitate. Did Dare tell her I'd gotten sick?

"Yes," I finally lie. "Perfectly fine."

"How about sleeping?" she continues. "Have you been sleeping well?"

No.

"Yes," I lie again. "Fine. I don't need any of your tea."

She smiles again, her teeth ever grotesque.

"That wasn't why I was asking. If you experience any... disturbances, do let me know."

Disturbances?

She glances at me knowingly before she shuffles away and I wonder what exactly she knows about me, and *how does she know it?*

I watch her disappear down the hall and it isn't until she's long gone that I realize that I have chills and that goose-bumps have lifted the hair on my neck.

I rub my arms and make my way quickly to the safety of my bedroom.

No one can see me.

I'm invisible.

There's a sheet and blood and water.

There are stones and moss and sand.

SeeMeSeeMeSeeMe.

But they don't.

Everyone bustles around, their faces turning into blurs.

"Help!" I scream.

But no one listens.

No one cares because I'm invisible.

I don't exist anymore.

I want to scream and howl at the sky, but it would do no good.

The night is a prison, a prison, a prison.

But the morning will kill me.

I know it.

I feel it.

I am.

I am.

I am.

I am lost.
And no one can save me.

Chapter Eighteen

I'm restless.

So very restless.

So I get dressed in a modest outfit, something befitting of a Savage so that Eleanor can't complain, slacks and a short-sleeved pink sweater. Afterward, I find Jones downstairs.

"Do you think you could drive me into town?" I ask him. His answer is immediate.

"Of course, miss."

I wait out front for the car, and as we're pulling away, down the drive, I have the oddest sensation... like I'm being watched.

The hair stands up on my neck, and I twist around to see out the rear window.

A curtain in the very top of Whitley falls closed, as though someone had been standing there.

As though someone *had* been watching me.

I swallow hard, and turn back around.

I'm in a car. No one can hurt me here.

That's what I tell myself as we drive into town.

"Where to, Miss Price?" Jones ask me when we reach the outskirts.

I don't know.

"Can you take me somewhere my mother used to go?" I ask hesitantly. Because I miss her. I want to feel close to her, even it's just an illusion.

Jones meets my eyes in the mirror, and his are sympathetic.

"Of course," he tells me, his gruff voice softening just a bit. "I know just the place."

The car weaves among the streets, and eventually comes to a stop outside of a church.

With a plain brick Gothic Revival exterior, the church looms against the cloudy sky, sort of severe and imposing.

I'm hesitant as I peer out the glass.

"It's the Church of St. Thomas of Canterbury," Jones tells me. "Your mother used to come here frequently."

That's a bit hard to believe, seeing how she wasn't catholic. I tell him so politely.

"She *was* catholic, miss," he insists. "And she did used to come here. I drove her myself."

I'll have to take him at his word, and I open the car door, stepping outside.

"I'll wait, miss,' he tells me, settling into the seat. I nod, and with my shoulders back, I walk straight to the doors.

Once inside, the demeanor of the church changes, from severe gothic, to lavishly decorated, firmly in line with Catholic tradition.

It feels reverent in here, holy and serene. And even if I'm not a religious person, I enjoy it.

The statues of saints and angels hanging on the walls are gilded and full of detail, including the crucifix of Christ at the front.

His face is pained, His hands and feet are bleeding.

I look away, because even still, it's hard for me to imagine such a sacrifice.

"Are you here for confession, child?"

A low voice comes from behind and I turn to find a priest watching me. His eyes are kind above his white collar, and it's the first real, sincere kindness I've seen since I've been in England.

Dare is kind, but our relationship is complicated.

Eleanor is severe, Sabine is mysterious, Jones is perfunctory. They all want something from me.

This man, this priest, is kind simply to be kind.

I swallow.

"I'm not catholic," I tell him, trying to keep my words soft in this grand place. He smiles.

"I'll try not to hold that against you," he confides, and he holds his hand out. I take it, and it's warm.

"I'm Father Thomas," he introduces himself. "And this is my parish. Welcome."

Even his hands are kind as he grasps mine, and I find myself instantly at ease for the first time in weeks.

"Thank you," I murmur.

"Would you like a tour?" he suggests, and I nod.

"I'd love one."

He doesn't ask why I'm here or what I want, he just leads me around, pointing out this artifact and that, this architecture detail or that stained glass window. He chats with me for a long time, and makes me feel like I'm the only person in the world, and that he has no place else to be.

Finally, when he's finished, he turns to me. "Would you like to sit?"

I do.

So he sits with me, and we're quiet for a long time.

"My mother used to come here, I'm told," I finally confide. "And I just wanted to feel like I'm near her."

The priest studies me. "And do you?"

My shoulders slump. "Not really."

"I've been here for a long time," he says kindly. "And I think I know your mother. Laura Savage?"

I'm surprised and he laughs.

"Child, you could be her mirror image," he chuckles. "It wasn't hard to figure out."

"You knew her?" I breathe, and somehow, I do feel closer to her, simply because he was.

He nods and looks towards Mary. "Laura is a beautiful soul," he says gently. "And I can see her in your eyes. Why didn't she come with you today?"

"She's gone," I say simply. "She died recently."

I don't mention that I killed her with a phone call, that it's my fault.

He blinks. "I'm so sorry. She's with the Lord now, though. She's at peace. Did she receive Last Rites, child?"

My breath leaves me. "I don't know. She couldn't have, I guess. She died in a car accident. Is that bad?"

Father Thomas rushes to reassure me. "No. In that circumstance, it is understandable. Don't fear, child. God in His merciful love isn't bound by sacraments. He blesses his children and forgives them, and bestows everlasting life to the faithful. Your mother was faithful."

I don't want to tell him that she wasn't a practicing Catholic, that I'd never even seen her attend a mass. Although now, the fact that she'd given Finn a St. Michael's medallion makes sense. I feel it now, chilling the skin on my chest.

"You must be very sad," he observes, and the way his face is turned in the light startles me, because I've seen him before and I didn't know until now.

"You were with Dare in the café the other day," I realize. "You were upset."

Father Thomas' eyes widen a bit, then he masks his expression. "It was nothing," he assures me. "We were just chatting over coffee. Nothing to be alarmed about."

But his eyes tell a different story.

The priest is lying, but why?

I pull away my hand and he notices.

"What is wrong, child?"

His demeanor is still soft, still gentle, still inviting, but I've been surrounded by secrets for so long that I can't accept that from a man of God. I tell him that.

He's pensive as he studies me.

"I understand, Calla. But you have to understand, too, that I'm told things in confidence. I have given my word, to God and to the members of my parish, that I won't break those confidences."

He's so kind, and his eyes are warm.

"I see you pray to St. Michael."

I hadn't even noticed that I'd pulled the medallion out of my shirt and have been turning it over in my hands.

"My mother gave it to my brother. He died, too. It was supposed to protect him…."

Father Thomas nods. "St. Michael will protect you, Calla. You just have to trust."

Trust.

That's actually a bit laughable in my current circumstances.

"Let's pray together, shall we?" he suggests, and I don't argue because it can't hurt.

Our voices are soft and uniform as they meld together in the sunlight,

In front of Christ on the Crucifix,

and the two Marys.

St. Michael the Archangel, defend us in battle. Be our defense against the wickedness and snares of the Devil. May God rebuke him, we humbly pray, and do thou, O Prince of the heavenly hosts, by the power of God, thrust into hell Satan, and all the evil spirits, who prowl about the world seeking the ruin of souls. Amen.

"Do you believe in evil?" I whisper when we're finished, and for some reason, my goose-bumps are back. I feel someone watching me, but when I open my eyes, Christ Himself stares at me. From his perch on the wall, his eyes are soft and forgiving while the blood drips from his feet.

"Of course," the priest nods. "There is good in the world, and there is evil. They balance each other out, Calla."

Do they?

"Because energy can't be destroyed?" I whisper. Because it goes from thing to thing to thing?'

The priest shakes his head. "I don't know about energy. I only know that there is good and evil. And we must find our own balance in it. You will find yours."

Will I?"

I thank him and stand up and he blesses me.

"Come back to see me," he instructs. "I've enjoyed our chat. If you're not catholic, I can't hear your confession, but I am a good listener."

He is. I have to agree.

I make my way out of the church, out of the pristine glistening silence, and when I step into the sun, I know I'm being watched.

Every hair on my head feels it, and prickles.

I turn, and the strange man is standing on the edge of the yard, just outside of the fence. He's watching me, his hands in his pockets, but I still can't see his face. His hood is pulled up yet again.

With my breath in my throat, I hurry down the sidewalk to the car, practically diving inside and slamming the door behind me.

"Has that guy been standing there long?" I ask Jones breathlessly.

"What guy, miss?" he asks in confusion, hurrying to look out the window.

I look too, only to find that he's gone.

Chapter Nineteen

Dare's hand closes over mine at dinner-time, as I'm reaching for the dining room door.

"Would you care for a walk?" he asks, his voice so low and rich.

I nod.

Because, God, I would.

Dare's hand is on the small of my back as he guides me to the veranda. We stop here, where the wisteria and plumeria grows, where I breathe it in and we stand staring at the stars.

"Do you remember Andromeda?" he asks, and I do remember that night back home. I remember sitting on the beach and his lecture about undying love, but now, it seems so relevant.

"I do," I tell him, and I lean into him, feeling his warmth and his strength. "And I believe you. Love is undying."

Finn.

My mom.

Undying.

He stares down at me, and then runs his fingers along my cheek. "Calla, you're so loved. You just don't know it right now. Please don't push me away."

I close my eyes, because the reasons that I was distancing myself somehow don't seem important anymore. But still.

Because secrets are the same thing as lies.

And I can't overlook his secrets.

"I know you think my mind is fragile," I tell him. "And I think you might be right."

He protests, but I shake my head. "No, I know you do. And that's fine. Because I still talk to Finn, Dare. I still pretend he's with me. A sane person wouldn't do that."

Dare swallows and holds my hand, and doesn't hesitate.

"They would if it helps," he tells me firmly. "You suffered a great loss, Calla. More than the average person could understand. If it helps you to pretend that Finn is here, then do it. As long as you know you're pretending."

I nod, because I do know, most of the time, at least where Finn is concerned.

But there's something else….something I won't mention.

The strange man in the hoodie.

Because I don't want to know if he's real.

"It's not fair to expect you to be with me when I'm in such an unbalanced state," I murmur, and everything in me wants him to argue, to protest, to pull me close.

But to my surprise, he doesn't.

He just nods. "I don't want to rush you," he says quietly. "When you're ready, you'll know."

His words graze my heart, but I brush them away.

This is what I asked for.

"Are you still drawing here?" I ask, trying to change the subject.

He nods. "Of course."

We keep walking, out of the gardens and down the path. The moon shines overhead, illuminating our steps.

"May I see your drawings?"

Dare smiles. "Of course. Would you like a new one?"

I remember posing for him.

When he drew me, painted me,

those feelings were so intimate and familiar,

I can't say no.

I nod. "Yes."

"I'll go get my sketch pad," he tells me. "Meet me in the library."

He leaves me at the door, and I curl up in the library and wait.

I wait in a window seat, bathed in the moonlight.

With my head pressed to the glass, I stare outside, out at the stables, at the trails, at the moors.

Something moves in the dark, and I focus, peering close.

The hoodie stands out in the night, the boy inside of it stealthy.

He steps out onto the trails and stares up at me,

But still I can't see his face.

I breathe and count,

One,

Two,

Three,

Four.

When I look again, he's gone.

He's not real.

Clearly.

"Are you ready?"

Dare stands behind me, his pad under his arm, a chair in his hand.

I try to settle my trembling lungs, and I nod.

"Yes."

Because this is real.

Dare is real.

My feelings for Dare are real.

"Tuck your legs beneath you," he whispers, moving to help me pose. His fingers are slender and strong, cool against my skin. "Hold your hand here," he shows me, moving my fingers to frame my cheek. "There. You're perfect."

I smile and he tells me to look into the distance, to look toward the stars outside.

I do, and I force myself to not look down,

Because I don't want to see anyone standing there.

The energy between Dare and I is thick. It snaps with tension, with unspoken words. I close my eyes and feel it, gliding over my skin like his pencils on the page.

I listen to the charcoal skimming the paper,

I hear Dare's shallow breaths as he concentrates.

Glancing at him, I watch as he shoves his hair out of his eyes with an impatient hand,

Rushing to get back to my picture.

He draws my leg,

He draws my eye,

He draws my lips.

And when he draws my lips, I get up from my seat, and I kneel in front of him.

I touch his with shaking fingers.

He closes his eyes, but then captures my hand with his own.

"Not 'til you're ready, Calla," he says, his words firm. "I can't... just not until you're ready."

I have to accept that because it's fair.

I can't waffle back and forth, I can't play games, even if it's with myself.

"Okay," I whisper. "I'm sorry."

"Don't be sorry, Cal," he tells me. "Just be ready soon. Please."

I have to smile at that, and I examine his picture.

I look sad, haunted, almost like a ghost as I perch in the window staring at the sky.

"Do I really look like that?" I ask dubiously and a bit disappointed.

"You're beautiful," he tells me and he believes it.

I rest my cheek against his knee.

"Is it awful being back here? I know you don't enjoy it."

But he came here for me. That says something.

It might say everything.

"It's not terrible," he answers. "You're here."

I am.

I'm here.

"What happened to you here," I ask him, bringing up a tender subject. He flinches, but looks away.

"Nothing you need to worry about."

"But I do," I tell him. "I worry."

He picks up my hand and holds it. "It isn't about me here," he says seriously. "It's about you."

I don't like that answer, but he walks me to my room, and kisses my forehead before he leaves me.

To my surprise, I sleep. And when I wake, the picture Dare drew is on my nightstand, but I don't remember putting it there.

Was he here while I slept?

I didn't hear him.

He's not at breakfast, so I search the grounds for him. The trails, the garage, the gardens. He's nowhere to be found, but Sabine is, of course.

"Hello, child," she greets me, her hands full of sod. I watch as she sifts the soil, as she plants and re-plants and prunes.

Why does everyone call me child?

"Good morning," I greet her. "Have you seen Dare?"

She shakes her head.

"He was out walking earlier," she offers. "But I think I saw him drive away."

I wonder where he goes every day.

I sink to my knees next to Sabine.

"What was his childhood like?" I ask, hoping she'll tell me what he won't. "You must know because you were his nanny."

"I was," she nods. "But Olivia was very much present, very much involved. Not like Eleanor was to your mother. Eleanor was detached. Olivia was loving. His mother loved him, child, so there's that."

But something is in her voice, something that tells me that Olivia loving him was his only thing.

"What about Richard?" I ask hesitantly. A cloud passes over Sabine's face.

"Richard never liked Dare," she answers honestly. "He thought Dare was competing for Olivia's affection, which is ridiculous. Dickie was cruel to Dare, but I did my best to protect him."

My heart twinges because something in the tone of her voice, lets me know that her best wasn't enough.

"What did he do to him?" I ask, and I'm honestly afraid to know.

She turns away.

"It doesn't matter anymore. It's past. It's done, and Dare paid for what he did."

This starts me, snapping my head back.

"What do you mean by that? What did Dare do?"

She shakes her head. "It's in the past. It doesn't matter."

But I know that it does.

It lives in Dare's face,

It haunts his eyes.

Secrets are the same as lies, and I must uncover his truth.

I leave Sabine behind, but I feel her watching me as I go.

Chapter Twenty

Once I'm in the house, morning light floods the dining room, and through the window, I watch Sabine walk through the gardens, her gait hunched and slow.

She examines something growing, something viridem, *green,* before she hunches over to look at it. Tearing a leaf off, she chews it thoughtfully, before turning her gaze to mine.

Her eyes meet mine through the glass, and then she walks away.

She knows I'm going to hunt, I realize. And she's not stopping me for a reason.

Maybe she wants me to know.

I find myself wandering through the hallways, ignoring the silence. The maids pretend they don't see me, and I steer far clear of the wing with Eleanor's office. I go down the East wing, a hall I haven't explored yet.

Immediately upon setting foot down the corridor, I feel a stillness, an unexplained quiet. I instantly feel like I'm in another place, somewhere remote, somewhere where there is no life. I don't even see any servants as I move over the polished marble floors.

I hesitate to even breathe loudly here, and I don't really know why.

I pause at a large carved double-door, and before I can think the better of it, I push it open.

It's someone's living quarters. I'm standing in a parlor area, in the middle of creams and beiges and blues. It's like someone threw up neutral colors and I spin in a circle, taking it in.

I've almost decided that it's a guest room, that's it's not worth exploring, when I see the edge of a picture in the next room. A portrait in a thick, gilded frame.

I cross the threshold and gaze up at the family in front of me.

Dare, his mother, and my uncle stare back down at me.

Dare is younger, of course. Much younger.

He looks to be only ten or so, thin and young, but those same dark eyes yawn from the photo, haunting and hurt. It's evident to anyone who looks at him that he's not happy. He shirks as far as he can from my uncle, although he allows his mother to wrap her arm around his shoulders. Her expression is soft, her eyes kind. I find myself wondering what in the world she's doing with Richard?

Because my uncle's eyes are hard as steel. He's got Eleanor's eyes and her rigid posture, too. He's imposing, he's stern. And I can tell he wasn't a nice person.

I find myself taking a step back, actually, which is silly.

And when I turn to look around the rest of the room, I still feel like he's watching me, which is silly too.

It's as quiet as the crypts in here, and part of it might be that I know that two of the three occupants of this suite are now dead. I saw their alcoves in the mausoleum, I traced their names beneath my fingers.

It's also apparent that Dare no longer occupies this room. He must've moved when his parents died, intent on avoiding memories.

I can't say that I blame him.

I can taste the memories in here in the air, and they aren't good.

Energy doesn't disappear.

There's a bad feeling in this room, although there's no tangible reason why.

There aren't any other photos. The dressers are all devoid of personal things, the walls filled only with ornamental décor. I glance into the closet and find it still full of clothing. Rows of suits, dresses and shoes. All exactly the way they'd been left. It has an eerie feel, as though it is frozen in time, and I turn to leave.

But I'm stopped by one thing.

A brown belt hangs on a hook just inside the door.

Normally, a belt wouldn't grab my attention, but this belt is old and battered, and covered in brown splotches.

It's old and battered in a house filled with exquisitely fine things.

But it's the fact that is battered that intrigues me. In a house of perfect, rich things, why would someone like Richard keep something so ratty?

I bend closer to examine it, and I trace the spots with my hand.

I yank my fingers away when I realize what the splotches are.

They're blood.

And I would bet any amount of money that the blood is Dare's.

I suck in a breath, my fingers fluttering to my chest as I imagine little Dare and those big sad eyes, and the huge man who used such a thick belt on such a tiny back.

In my head, I see Richard, swinging the belt, high and hard, and I see Dare fall to his knees, his head bowed, his mouth clenched tightly closed to avoid screaming.

He's stubborn and he won't cry, and I can't stop the visions in my head.

I don't want to imagine it, but the pictures still come and I can hear a woman crying. Dare's mother cries for Richard to stop, and he throws her off. She hits the wall behind the bureau, slamming into it hard enough to knock the picture from the wall.

The room swirls and the nausea returns and I fall to my knees, sucking in air.

What is happening to me?

Am I really seeing this?

I squeeze my eyes closed, trying to find solace in the dark, trying to close out the horror of this room.

But I can't.

Because Richard did this to Dare. I'm not imagining it. He hurt Dare over and over throughout the years and nobody stopped it, nobody could.

I tried my best to protect him.

But Sabine failed.

A whisper hisses around me, from the corners, from the ceiling, from the sky. *He did this. HeDidThisHeDidThisHeDidThis.*

The whisper turns to a roar and it overwhelms me, and I squeeze my eyes closed to block it out.

When I open them again, the room is dark.

Someone is sitting in the chair across the room, half hidden in the shadows.

"What are you doing in here?" Dare asks me, unmoving. His hands are on his thighs and he looks like he's waiting.

Waiting for me to wake up.

I blink the sleep away, trying to determine how long I've been here.

I scramble to my feet and fly into Dare's arms, surprising him with all my weight.

"I'm so sorry," I whisper to him over and over and he stares down at me like I'm the crazy person I am.

I'm dizzy, but I don't care.

All that matters is that Dare isn't little anymore, and he's in my arms and I'll never let anyone hurt him like that again.

"I'm so sorry he did that to you," I tell him, and his eyes widen before he looks away.

"I don't know what you mean."

His words are stilted, closed.

"My uncle hurt you," I say firmly. "I know he did. And God, I'm so sorry, Dare."

He's so leonine, even in the dark, graceful and strong. I stare at him helplessly as he tries to pretend that it's not a big issue, that he wasn't beaten as a child.

"You shouldn't have come in here," he says quietly. "There's nothing in here to see."

There was one thing.

A blood-stained belt.

And a whisper: *He did this.*

I pause, studying Dare's shadowed face. He's impassive, hiding his thoughts, but I've got to ask.

"My uncle was a horrible person," I tell him desperately, trying to make a dent in in his impassive face, the face that is so good at hiding things. "And Eleanor is terrible. You never knew my mother, so maybe you think all Savages are that way… you think they're terrible, and so you think I'm a hateful person now."

He's taken aback by this, but he stops trying to push me away.

"I don't think you're a hateful person," he argues, and his hands are limp at his sides. "I never thought that."

"Are you sure?" I ask him bluntly. "Because now that we're here at Whitley, you've changed."

"That's not true," he denies somewhat hotly, then tempers his tone. "You told me you wanted space, I'm giving it to you. Be careful what you wish for, Calla."

"You've been hurt here," I tell him. It's a statement, not a question, and I'm doing my best not to let his words hurt me. "In this room. At the hands of people related to me. I'm really sorry about that. God, I'm sorry."

Dare's handsome face shutters closed, and any trace of softness is gone.

"Don't feel sorry for me," he says icily. "People generally deserve what they get."

"What the hell does that mean?" I ask in confusion. "That's ridiculous."

He shakes his head. "It's just the truth. But not with you. You don't deserve any of it." He pauses. "Are you coming?"

He obviously doesn't want to leave me in here alone, so I trail behind, closing the door behind me.

I start to walk in the opposite direction, toward my room, but Dare stops me with a hand on my arm.

"Wait. I want to show you something."

"You do?"

"Yeah. You need to see it."

Confused, intrigued, and a bit scared, I follow him through the halls of the East wing, along back corridors and up old stairs to the attic. As we walk, I swear I can hear whispers... all around, coming from the floors and the nooks and the crannies.

Secrets.

Secrets.

Secretsssssssssss.

But of course there are no voices.

I'm imagining it all.

The problem is, as each day goes by, I'm not sure what I'm imagining anymore and what's real.

Once we're standing in the dark room, I take a deep breath and look around.

Old furniture, boxes, crates, and picture frames are stacked as far as I can see. It's clearly an old storage place, and not even maids come up here. There's a thick layer of dust everywhere.

Dare turns on a light, and leads me through the clutter.

He takes me to a back corner, where a massive desk sits amid a makeshift office space.

"Yours?" I raise my eyebrow. "I can't picture you up here."

208

He rolls eyes and shakes his head. "No, it's not mine.

The floor creaks beneath my feet, and when I look down, I find a stack of framed pictures... of Dare, of Eleanor, of my grandfather, of Dare's mother. The glass on each one is shattered.

Who did that?

"Why did you bring me here?" I whisper, and I suddenly am on edge. Something is here, something huge, something I need to know.

Dare looks away, his expression troubled.

"Look at the bottom of that pile, Calla." He motions to a stack of envelopes on the desk. It's a thick stack, held together with a rubber band.

With hesitant fingers, I sift through the paper.

I'm startled to find letters to my father that I've written over the past couple of weeks, unopened, unstamped, unsent. My appalled gaze meets Dare's.

"If my letters haven't been mailed, then how does my father know I'm ok?" I ask slowly, trying to imagine why Sabine wouldn't have mailed them.

"He doesn't," Dare nods. "That's the thing."

"I... I don't know what is happening," I say in a broken whisper, and I look away, around the room, my gaze coming to a stop on the chair behind the desk.

A gray hoodie hangs there, its cuffs dragging on the floor.

I've seen that hoodie before, on the man no one can see but me.

My heart pounds.

My mind races.

"I don't want to be here anymore," I admit aloud. I want to be home, I want to be safe, I want to be away from *all of this.*

"Then go," Dare's words are soft, and his eyes are softer, liquid black, like a starry night.

And in this moment, I know I can't leave him.

"I would never leave you," I tell him, and I mean every word.

Dare's head snaps back and he gets to his feet, circling the desk and standing in front of me. I breathe in his scent and his uncertainty and I match his gaze.

"This isn't about me, Calla," he answers, his hand on my arm. "If you need to leave, you should go."

"I won't leave you alone."

In my head, I remember the little boy he used to be, the little boy in the picture, and the pain that used to live in his eyes. He was so small, so vulnerable, so very alone. He's learned to hide it all now, but that makes me even sadder.

His smile is grim. "I'm always alone, Calla. I'm used to it."

And somehow, I believe it. Regardless of who he surrounds himself with, he's alone because he hasn't let anyone in.

"You don't have to be," I offer. "I can help."

Save me, and I'll save you.

He smiles but it doesn't reach his eyes and he bends, his lips touching my neck as he murmurs into my ear.

"Run, little mouse. The hawk is coming, and you're going to get eaten."

My breath comes in spurts as he leaves me amid the chaos of the attic. I listen for his steps on the stairs, and only when I can't hear him anymore do I feel comfortable leaving myself. I tuck my father's letters into my pocket and creep down the stairs, hiding them in my room before dinner.

Chapter Twenty-One

I have Jones drive me back to the church before dinner, and to my relief, Father Thomas is there, kneeling at the feet of Jesus.

When I come in, he gets to his feet, his robes heavy around his ankles.

"Calla," he greets me warmly, and he is sincerely happy to see me.

"Do you know what happened at Whitley?" I ask him without preamble.

He hesitates and looks away, but finally he answers.

"Yes," he acknowledges. "It was terrible."

We walk together, he and I, toward the front where we sit on a pew. My back is as stiff as Eleanor's, my breath hesitant as I wait.

"Can you tell me?" I ask and he looks up at God.

"I think," he replies slowly. "That some things are left unsaid, and perhaps actions are your true answers."

I'm confused and I tell him that and he nods.

"You wonder what happened to Adair. But to be honest, the only thing that matters is who Adair is today. You know who he is, and that's what's important."

But I know what I know.

I want to know what I don't.

"Eleanor Savage hid it," he nods. "She doesn't wish for it to be known or talked about. Perhaps that's why you encounter so many walls at Whitley."

"Father," I say slowly, watching his face as I speak. "Would you believe me if I said I have dreams... dreams about things that have happened?"

"What do you mean, my child?"

So then, because he's a priest and he has vowed to hold things confidential, to his parish and to God, I tell him.

I tell him all of it, as though I'm confessing to some great sin.

"I don't ask for the dreams," I tell him desperately. "And sometimes, I'm not sure if I'm crazy. Maybe I'm imagining what I see."

Just like I imagine my dead brother.

The priest sighs and he holds my hand, his grip so warm and sincere.

"I don't know how to explain it," he says finally. "But your dream, in this case, is true. There was a terrible thing that happened... with Dare and Richard and Olivia. Richard was cruel and he damaged Adair in a thousand different ways. And one day, Dare couldn't take it anymore. But he paid for that, my dear. A thousand times over."

"How?" I ask, fear in my tone and stilting my words.

"If Dare wants you know, he'll tell you," Father Thomas answers carefully. "Until then, you should know, he's a good boy."

I know he's good. I know his eyes, I know his heart.

He's too good for me, even though he thinks otherwise.

Even if he thinks he's a monster.

"Few know what happened," the priest continues. "But those that do whisper that Adair could be dangerous. Don't believe them."

I've done terrible things, Dare said once.

You're not safe.

I wrap my mind around these things, or try to. But it's too much, too much, too much to focus on.

"There's something else, Father," I continue, speaking softly because Jesus is watching me from his bloody perch on the wall.

The priest waits.

"I see someone," I say hesitantly, because I know how insane it sounds. "When I'm out walking, the last time I was here, on the grounds of Whitley. A man in a gray hooded sweatshirt. He watches me, and he wants something from me."

The father is interested by this. "Does he speak to you?" he asks, my hand still cradled in his.

"No. He seems to want me to find something, but I don't know what it is."

The father peruses me, his expression gentle.

"You've been through a great deal, Calla," he says, his words so understanding. "Perhaps you're still trying to figure it all out."

I want to slip into the floor because he's basically saying I'm crazy.

"I'm not crazy, am I?" I ask and he shakes his head.

"Of course not," he says firmly.

"Does it have to do with Dare's secret?" I ponder and the priest shrugs.

"I don't know."

He doesn't treat me like I'm crazy or like the things I'm saying are so preposterous. He just listens and smiles and holds my hand.

He's a true comfort and I tell him so.

Today, when I leave, the boy in the sweatshirt is nowhere in sight.

Thank God.

At dinner, Eleanor turns to me.

"Don't forget, the event is tomorrow night. Your dress has been delivered, along with your jewels and shoes. You are up for it, I presume?"

Like always, her question isn't a question.

I nod. "Of course."

She nods back and we continue eating, and Dare is late again.

This time, Eleanor looks up. "Don't bother sitting down," she snaps. "I've warned you before. If you're late, don't bother coming."

Without a word, he turns and walks out.

"Excuse me," I murmur, and I follow.

I hear Eleanor calling me, but I don't turn around.

Dare's strides are long, but I run to catch him.

"Wait," I say breathlessly, and I pull at his arm.

He's patient as he stares down at me.

"Let's go eat in town," I suggest. "Together."

He smiles at this and glances at the dining room.

"You know she'll be upset if we do."

"I don't care," I answer honestly.

We ride to town in Dare's car.

"Will you be all right tomorrow night?" he asks. "You won't know anyone."

"I'll know you," I tell him. "You'll be there, won't you?"

"If you want me to be."

"I do."

"Consider it done, then," he says quietly, and he motions for a waiter. "She'll have dessert," he tells the skinny man.

I've done a terrible thing, he said.

"What did you do?" I ask bluntly, as I take a bite of cake. "What is your secret?'

Dare startles, then almost laughs.

"It doesn't matter anymore," he answers. "Because you're here and the past is gone."

I almost believe that it's that easy.

We finish our dinner, and drive back to Whitley and when we're in the car, Dare hums.

I close my eyes and listen, and soak in the sound. I think it's the song he played on the piano, and when we get home, I ask him to play.

So he does.

The salon is quiet and dark, and his notes drift on the air like snow.

I sit next to him, content to soak in the sound, his scent, his air.

If he's the air, I'll happily breathe it.

I almost float away on his song, and when he's done, the silence is loud.

He walks me to my room.

"Some things are best left alone," he reminds me at my door.

"But what it…"

He shakes his head, interrupting me.

"Trust me."

I wish I could.

But *he did a terrible thing.*

And I have to know.

Chapter Twenty-Two

When I stare into the mirror, a woman looks back. A woman draped in red silk, a woman with thick lashes and full lips.

"You look beautiful," Finn tells me as he straightens the clasp of my necklace.

"Thank you, but anyone would look good in this dress."

He can't argue because he's not real.

"What do you think will happen tonight? A dance? A sacrifice? Will you have to drink goat's blood or bathe with a thousand virgins?"

I roll my eyes.

"Doubtful. But if you were here, you'd have to do the Macarena."

He grabs his chest and falls onto the bed. "I would refuse."

"Then it's a good thing you aren't here."

"You've got this," he announces. "Even without me."

I'm not so sure.

But I have no choice other than to just go.

I find the great room and discover that it's been transformed into a ballroom.

It's draped with white tulle and sparkling lights, with candles and pungent flowers.

I find Eleanor, dressed in a conservative black dress and pearls, chatting with a small group of men in suits. Her lip is as stiff as her back, and I decide she must never relax. I scan the room for the most important face, and it doesn't take long to find him.

Dare is in the back, sitting at a table in the shadows.

He's here just like he promised.

He's watching me, his dark gaze impenetrable. In his black tux, he's impossibly handsome and I find I can't look away.

He's got a glass tumbler in his hand and he sips at the amber liquid, and it looks to be something strong, like scotch.

My breath is shallow and I can't quite catch it. I take a step in his direction, then another, then I pause. Because his expression is so unreadable.

Without breaking our gaze, he thunks the glass down on the nearest side-table, and then turns his back, walking to the open veranda doors. He steps into the night, and I desperately want to follow him.

Not just because I want to be with him, but because it's away from here, away from Eleanor, away from the prying stares of the people who are wondering who I am.

But I'm stopped by well-meaning snobby people who want to chat.

Where are you from?

Will you be attending Cambridge?

Will you be at the polo match this weekend?

Will you come to tea?

Eleanor, I see, manages to skirt the crowd and sit alone in the corner with a cup of what looks to be tea. I wonder if it is spiked. Then I wonder what the purpose of this party is at all... other than to force me into interacting with people.

Why would she do this? She has to know I'm not ready.

Dare's words come back to haunt me.

The hawk is coming, and you're going to get eaten.

Who is the hawk? Him?

I twist to find him, and he's still on the veranda, joined by a blonde girl. She knows him, that much is apparent. She's holding onto his arm and my belly tightens, bile rising in my throat. She's possessive and he doesn't push her away.

I turn my back.

Eleanor is watching Dare, too, a look of mild distaste on her face, but it's the same look she always has with him. She hates him for some reason, that much is apparent. But why?

I'm being watched, and I scan the sea of faces to find Sabine shuffling along the back, dressed in black.

Her eyes have found me in the madness and *we're all a bit mad, aren't we?*

I swallow hard, and turn away. There's no one here I can trust.

No one.

No one.

No one.

I make a run for the bathroom.

Because I need to hide.

Once inside the quiet powder room, I sink to a seat on a velvet bench, my breath shaky.

I don't belong here.

I don't belong here.

"You don't belong here, do you?"

It's like the calm voice reads my mind.

The voice belongs to the voluptuous blonde who was hanging on Dare's every word.

Startled, I look up at her.

She stares back at me coolly, but not unkindly.

"You're wearing my dress."

My heart hammers. *This dress was made for Miss Aimes, but we can make her another.*

"Uh," I stammer. "I'm sorry, I didn't realize."

She shrugs and adjusts her lipstick in the mirror. She's wearing a black dress instead, something that hugs her curves. She didn't need this red dress. She's perfect in anything she wears. I can see that much.

"I'm Ashley," she tells me, and she smiles in the mirror. "And I hate these things too. I can help you, you know."

"You can?"

She nods.

"Let's get out of here. I'll show you where I hide during these horrid things."

Her smile is one of camaraderie, and any port in a storm.

I follow her right out of the ballroom, and I feel Dare's eyes on us as we go.

When we're in the driveway, she turns to me.

"Maybe you should've brought a wrap. You might get cold."

But she puts the top down on her car anyway, and the breeze is cold as we speed through the night, away from Whitley.

"Where are we going?" I finally ask her, relieved to be so far away.

She glances at me.

"Someplace you should see. If you think you want to be with Dare, you should know all about him."

There's something in her voice now, something rigid, and I startle, because maybe I shouldn't have chosen this port.

She turns down a dark road, a quiet lane, and then we pull to a stop in front of an old, crumbling building.

"Come on," she calls over her shoulder, traipsing up the steps in her black high heels. I feel clumsy as I follow, and she doesn't slow down. The sign by the door says Oakdale Sanitarium and I freeze.

"What is this place?" I whisper as she opens the door.

"You'll have to see it to believe it," she murmurs.

In front of us, a long hallway yawns farther than I can see, the walls crumbling with age, the lights dim when she flips a switch.

There's no one here, but I can hear moans, screams, whimpers.

"I don't understand," I feel like whimpering myself. Ashley rolls her eyes.

"Do you really think someone like Dare is without baggage? Grow up, little girl."

She pushes open the doors as we pass, and they're all empty, every single one.

But I feel presences here,

Ugliness.

When we're almost at the end of the hall, Ashley turns to me, her gaze ugly now and I should've known.

"His mother was here for years," she tells me, like she's confiding a secret. "After what Dare did, it's no wonder."

Her eyes are so knowing and I close my eyes,

Because the screams are deadening.

I my head, I see Dare and he's so small.

He stands above a bed, hovering above two sleeping people.

Something is shiny in his hand, something flashes in the night,

And I try to tell him no, to warn him not to move,

But of course he can't hear.

Then there's screaming and blood.

My uncle is bloody in the bed, and a dark-haired woman is screaming.

I see the alcove in the crypts and his name is carved in the stone.

Richard William Savage II.

Dare's eyes are wide and dark,

Haunted,

Haunted,

Haunted.

I gasp and open my eyes and my reality isn't any better.

I'm not in an abandoned clinic any longer, and I probably never was.

I'm in a small but well-appointed room,

A room in a facility.

A room frozen in time.

The room is lined with pictures of Dare.

Ranging from toddlerhood, to primary school, to secondary school, to University, Dare smiles at me from the walls. When he was small, he smiled, but over time,

More and more,

He became haunted and sad.

The change in his eyes is startling.

And then,

Suddenly,

A woman is in front of me, dark-haired. She has Dare's eyes, and I know who she is.

Olivia Savage.

I hesitate, and she smiles.

"Are you here to bring me my son?" she asks politely. "The boy from the pictures? He did something bad, but he's sorry."

I can't breathe.

I can't breathe.

I stare at her face, at her smile, and at the unlocked door.

She reaches out her hand to me,

And I reach to take it,

Then I open my eyes.

I didn't even know they were closed.

I'm in the powder room again,

And Ashley Aimes is in front of me,

Annoyance on her pretty face,

And *we never left this room.*

We. Never. Left.

"What is wrong with you? My lord, you need help."

She stalks away and I struggle to breathe, trying like hell to grasp reality.

What is happening to me?

I do need help.

I need Dare.

Because he was so hurt, and I'm hurting him now, more and more each day as I keep pushing him away.

He didn't deserve that.

He doesn't deserve *this*.

I'm reeling,

I'm reeling.

The room presses down on me, swirling and bending and stifling. I lunge for the door, and barge through the people and to Dare on the veranda.

Ashley is with him now, telling him of my break-down and he turns to me, his beautiful face frozen and afraid.

"Dare... I..."

Tears streak my cheeks and he grabs me, turning his back on Ashley.

"You're not a monster," I whisper. "You're not."

Without looking back, he leads me away,

Out of the ballroom,

Away from all of the watchful eyes.

"I saw what happened," I whisper, and I turn into his tuxedo jacket, hiding my face. "Am I crazy? I saw what you did. I know your mom isn't dead."

"You're not crazy," his words are gentle, and it's a soft tone I haven't heard from him in awhile. My walls come crumbling down, and I cry.

The next few minutes are a blur.

I reach for him,

he pulls me close.

His breath is sweet,

his shirt is starchy and smells of rain,
musk,
and man.
His hands are everywhere,
Firm,
Strong,
And perfect.
His lips are full,
Yet
Soft.
His tongue finds mine,
Moist,
Minty.
His heart beats hard,
The sound harsh in the dark,
And I cling to his chest,
Whispering his name.
"Dare, I…"

"Let's leave this room," he suggests. "Let's leave it all behind."

So we do.

Chapter Twenty-Three

He takes my hand and I follow him,

Because I'd follow him to the ends of the earth.

I know that now, and I tell him.

He turns to me, his eyes so stormy and dark.

He scoops me up in my red silk dress, and he's striding through the hallways of Whitley.

His room is dark and masculine, the bed looming against the wall. We tumble into it, and his hand is behind my head as I fall into the pillow.

Our clothing is stripped away and our skin is hot and flushed and alive.

I'm alive.

Dare lives free.

We breathe that freedom in, and he strokes his fingers against me, into me, deep inside and I gasp and sigh and quiver.

"I... yes." I murmur into his ear.

Consequences can be damned.

I don't care who he is.

I don't care what he's done.

He's here.
He makes me feel.
I want him.
He wants me.
So he takes me.
There is no pain.
He's inside and fills me, and his hands...
work magic.
His lips...
breathe life into me,
Filling me,
Creating me.
I call his name.
He calls mine.
I'm intoxicated by the sound, by the cadence, by
the beat.
His heart matches, in firm rhythm.
We're so very alive,
And together.
Our arms and legs tangle.
Our eyes meet and hold.
His stare into mine as he slides inside,
Then out.
I clutch his shoulders,
To hold him close.
He shudders,
The moonlight spills from the window,
Onto my skin,
And his.

His eyes, framed by thick black lashes, close.

He sleeps.

But he wakes in the night and we're together again, and again and again.

Each time it's new,

Each time is reverent and raw and amazing.

In the morning, as he is bathed in sunlight, Dare finally looks away. Shame in his eyes, guilt in his heart.

"She's dead now," Dare tells me when I ask again about his mom. "But she didn't die with Richard."

I don't ask about Richard,

I don't ask Dare to confirm what I know.

He killed his step-father,

And it made his mother crazy.

"Do you see now why I don't deserve you?" he asks, and his voice is almost fragile.

You're better than I deserve.

He's said it before, over and over, and I never knew what he meant.

I know it now, but it's still not true. I'm not better than he deserves, not by a long shot, not ever.

He sits straight up in bed.

"Come with me," he says suddenly. "Let's leave this place behind. You don't need to be here to recover. We can find peace and quiet anywhere. We go can together, Calla."

But I pause and my hesitancy is answer enough, and Dare's face falls.

"You're not ready to leave," he realizes.

"It's not that," I say slowly. "I'll go... if there's nothing else I need to know. Was this your only secret, Dare?" My hands trail along his chest, feeling his heart where it beats just for me. "Was this what you didn't want me to know?"

He shakes his head.

"No."

"There's more?"

He nods.

The room swirls again and again, and I hold my hands out.

I'm falling,

Falling,

Falling, and I don't know where I'll land.

The world is a stage and we all act falsely upon it.

The die has been cast,

Has been cast,

Has been cast.

I feel it,

The truth.

It's coming,

And it's dark,

And I won't like it.

I feel it.

I feel it.

We all have our parts to play, and I'll play mine well.

But what is it?

I concentrate, and think,
And more will come.
We're all a bit mad, aren't we?
Yes.

Chapter Twenty-Four

Things change with Dare.

He's still *my Dare*.

He's still reserved, yet sweet.

Strong, yet vulnerable.

He's guarded now, as though he's waiting for something terrible,

the other shoe to drop.

It makes me uneasy, and even though we're together night after night, I feel him growing away from me. It's enough to make me panic.

At dinner, he watches me.

During the day, he walks with me.

He sketches me.

He loves me.

But there's always something in his eyes, something hidden, something he won't share.

"It's not time," he always says when I ask. "But soon."

I feel like I should be progressing.

I should be growing.

I should be recovering.

But I'm not.

And the more I think about, the more I've decided why.

So in my room, after I've sipped at my tea, I know there's something I have to do. Something I've been putting off, something that makes my heart heavy.

"Finn," I say aloud, and instantly he's beside me.

He grins at me with his crooked grin, and my heart breaks with what I have to do.

"I can't see you anymore," I tell him sadly, and he looks away.

"I know."

"How am I supposed to be without you?" I ask quietly, picking up his hand. It's pale, and I know that freckle on his knuckle. He's had it since we were five.

He shrugs, and he tries to act nonchalant, but this moment is huge and he knows it.

"I don't know, Cal. What's anyone to do without me?" He grins and I cry, because I can't help it.

Because he's my other half, but *I have to be sane.*

"Don't cry," he says softly and he pats my back. "It'll be ok. It'll all be ok."

"It won't," I sniffle through my tears. "There are so many things I don't understand, and I can't work through it without *you.* "

He laughs now and stands up, his brown curls flopping over his eye. "That's absurd," he tells me and humor makes his voice thin. "You can do anything, Calla."

"I can't keep saying goodbye to you," I tell him and he's knows that I'm right. "Every time it rips the band-aid off, and you take a piece of my heart with you."

"So quit talking to me," he tells me simply, looking through to my soul. "You're my sister and you'll always be my sister. I don't need to be with you for you to know that."

I close my eyes.

"I can't."

His hand is on mine.

"You can."

There's silence, and his hand is cold.

His hand is cold because he's dead.

"Good night, sweet Finn," I whisper. "Good night."

I see his headstone, the dragonfly, the grave.

His hand is gone.

I open my eyes.

I'm alone.

I take out paper and a pen, and I write yet another letter to my father. I don't know why I continue because he never answers.

But I write and write, and when I'm finished, I give it to Sabine.

"You'll mail it this time, won't you?" I ask. She nods.

"It'll go out in the morning. I'll make you a cup of tea now, child. And I'll bring it to you in the salon."

I sit and I wait, and while I do, I have a visitor.

Father Thomas.

Jones show him in, and I smile.

"It's good to see you, Father." Because it is.

He sits with me in the sun, chatting and holding my hand. He's a soothing presence, and I soak it in while I can.

He stares out the windows at the gardens, at the statues and flowers and paths. "Do you like it here?" he asks quietly, and I have to shake my head.

"No. I thought I might get used to it, but I find that I'm really not."

Father Thomas smiles. "It's a daunting place," he agrees. "And it's not for everyone. Maybe it's time for you to leave, child."

I look away. "I know. But I don't know where to go."

The priest cocks his head, the light shining in his eyes. "Go home, child."

Home.

The place where memories plague me. Where Finn's shoes and his journal and his unmade bed wait, the things he'll never use again.

Home, a place surrounded by death.

"Maybe," I whisper.

He smiles. "Let me pray with you before I go."

I nod, and he rests his hand on my forehead.

"Through this holy anointing may the Lord in his love and mercy help you with the grace of the Holy Spirit. May the Lord who frees you from sin save you and raise you up."

He removes his hand. "Amen."

"Amen," I murmur too.

I walk Father Thomas out and he waves as he drives away.

Then I roam the grounds, because Dare isn't here and I'm restless.

The mausoleums are quiet, the gardens are still.

And then,

There's the boy in the hoodie.

He stands just on the inside of the fence,

And his head is tilted just enough that I can't see his face.

I step toward him, and he steps toward me.
His face is dark, and I peer toward him,
Then another step.
Then another.
He stops.

"Who are you?" I shout, and my words are carried on the wind. He cocks his head but doesn't answer, although there's a low growl in his throat.

"What do you want?"

He's calm, his head is down. But his arm comes up,

And he points at me.

He wants me.

I run to the house without looking back.

Chapter Twenty-Five

I feel like I need to go home.

I feel it tugging at me, pulling.

I'm not safe here.

But yet, I can't leave Dare.

I can't leave him because he's mine.

The Dare he shows the world is different from *my Dare*, the one who holds me in his arms. I feel his secrets, though, through my skin, through my bones, and that's not something he can fake.

I ache for him to take me into his confidence, to trust me that much, but he hasn't yet. There's something left to know… an answer left to be had.

I need to find it.

I don't make it far before Sabine finds me.

It's like she was waiting just for me.

"It's time to read your cards again," she tells me, as though it's not one in the morning, as though it's such a normal thing.

I start to shake my head, but she won't hear it.

"It's important," she insists.

Her gnarled fingers sink into my flesh, her fingernails biting into my muscle. I let her take me to her room, to where it's dark and the moonlight is shining onto the table.

The cards are already spread out, in the same weird cross, the gold gleaming garishly in the night.

"You started without me," I point out softly. She glances at me, and sits down.

"I read them every day," she admits. "But recently, the night of the party, they changed."

The night I was with Dare.

The night I found out what he did.

Of course.

Everything changed that night.

I felt it.

"Pick up a card," she tells me. "The one on top."

I do. It's cool beneath my fingers.

A priest rises against a stained glass window.

"The hierophant," Sabine whispers. "The teacher. It means you must listen to me now, the time to teach is here."

"Teach me what?" I ask, my voice the merest of whispers. I'm scared now, at her tone, of these cards, of this place. I was wrong to stay here. I know that now.

There was a fork in the road, and I chose the wrong path.

"I have to teach you what you need to know. Your mother wouldn't let me, she left. But you're here and you must learn from me, child."

Oh my god. This just gets weirder and weirder. I start to get up.

"I'm going back to bed now," I tell her. "This just got too strange for me."

"Sit," Sabine directs, her voice stern and loud and unarguable.

I sit.

I can do nothing else.

Sabine sifts through the cards, her eyes moving so fast that I see them working back and forth, faster and faster, like she's experiencing a dream.

Finally, she looks up at me.

"Your mind is a gift," she says simply. "But you have to learn from it, or you will go crazy from it."

Her words don't make any sense.

I stare at her, not comprehending.

Her eyes contain a thousand lives.

I stare into them all, into her gypsy mind, and I see that she believes everything she's saying as truth.

"It's as much a part of life as the wind or the sun," she says in her husky, old voice. "It's not strange, it's not abnormal. We know what happens while others don't."

She pauses and looks out the windows, out at the black waving grasses of the dark moors.

"You can see things," she says finally. "Little things, things that might seem like dreams. You might feel sick afterward, you might have a headache. You might even feel crazy. You're not."

The crypts.

Dare's parents' room.

The Sanitarium and Dare's mother.

I try to hide my expression, but Sabine has already seen and she smiles with her grotesque teeth.

"See? You know what I'm speaking of."

"I'm not….it's not… real."

She cocks her head.

"Your dreams are important. Even when you're awake."

I want to scream from the insanity of it, because it does feel like a nightmare.

"Why am I here?" I ask her, because all along, I've felt like there was a bigger reason.

"To recover," she tells me, but I know there's more.

She hands me a necklace. It gleams gold in the night, a locket with a flower engraved on the front. A calla lily.

I try to open it, but it's locked.

"It's your secret," Sabine tells me, her dark eyes so knowing.

"Why do I have a secret?"

"Because we don't get to choose," she answers cryptically. "Because we pay for the sins of those who came before us."

With a sigh, I leave her room on shaky legs and retreat back to my own. Against my better judgment, I wear the locket to bed, and it nestles against my breast as I drift to sleep.

And that is the first night I dream of her.

Of Olivia.

Of Dare's mother.

She wears a white nightgown, filmy and light, and she stands at the window.

Her hair falls down her back dripping wet, and her figure is small and slight.

She turns, her eyes just like Dare's, and so very sad.

"I don't know where I am," she whispers, and her eyes beg me for help. "I don't know."

She turns away, looking out the window at the sea.

Behind us, the waves crash.

Pictures of Dare hang on the wall, from infant to adulthood.

She looks at them longingly.

"Can you bring him to me?"

I want to answer her, but I can't.

My lips are frozen.

My words are ice.

I can't melt them.

I can't bring him.

Save me, save you.

I wake in a pool of sweat, alone.

"Finn?" I call out, desperate to feel calm, but he doesn't answer.

There will come a day when I don't, he'd once said. Is today that day?

The moonlight shines on my nightstand, and Sabine's box of tea sits in the light. I grab it up and make a cup.

I have to be calm,

I have to be calm.

This must be the way.

The tea creates oblivion and I sleep for hours and hours. When I'm finally up and around the next afternoon, Sabine finds me in the library.

"Did you wear the locket to bed?" she asks.

I stare at her, annoyed.

"I dreamed about Olivia Savage. Is that what you want to hear?"

Something passes through Sabine's eyes and I can't read it.

"What did you dream?"

"Not much," I have to admit. "I just saw her face. She had pictures of Dare on the wall. I could see the sea through the window. It's like she doesn't know where Dare is. She keeps asking for me to bring him to her."

She nods now, satisfied. "That's enough for now."

Enough for what?"

But I'm afraid to ask.

"A letter came for you today," she tells me and hands me a battered envelope.

I rip it open to find my father's handwriting.

It's time to come home, he says simply.

I think he might be right.

Soon.

It's time to go home soon.

I leave Sabine in her room, and I search for Dare.

I find him in the secret garden alone.

My heart jumps when I see him, at the way he leans against an angel statue so irreverently, at the familiarity in his eyes when he sees me. I fight the urge to leap into his arms, but of course I don't, because the warmth in his eyes has cooled.

"What are you doing out here?" he asks, so reserved.

I'm flustered.

"Hunting for you."

"I'm not good for you," he offers. "Maybe you should stop hunting for me."

My heart twinges.

"Never."

His expression falters.

"You need to let me figure out what's good for me," I add.

He looks at me sadly. "I can't. You don't know all of the facts."

"So tell me."

"I can't do that, either."

We're at an impasse, a fork in the road.

There are two roads, and I always take the wrong one.

"You'll destroy me," I remember Sabine's foreboding words. Dare closes his eyes, and nods.

"What does that mean?" My voice is raw.

There is pain in Dare's eyes, real pain.

The kind of pain that can't be hidden, can't be contained.

"I want you to know," he tells me, each word an honest rasp.

"But you can't tell me," I guess. He nods.

"Not yet. You'll come to in it in order."

In order.

In order.

In order.

Things must happen in order, Calla? Can't you see? Can't you see?

I remember Finn's cries from before, but before what?

Time is blurring now, blending, and I can't make sense of anything.

I'm standing on the cliffs, I'm staring at the ocean, but I'm not.

It's Finn.

But it was me.

Cars.

Blood.

Sirens.

Darkness.

Good night, sweet Finn. Good night, good night.

Protect me, St. Michael.

Protect me,

Protect me.

My mind can't take the stress,

It can't take the flex.

My mind is an elastic band,

And it's getting ready to break.

He'll be your downfall, child.

It's the first thing that makes sense.

Chapter Twenty-Six

I sit in Olivia's room, her locket in my hands.

It's gold, it's delicate, it's real. It's cool in my hands.

I concentrate on it, on the etched calla lily.

Symbolic? Ironic? Coincidental?

Nothing is a coincidence in this house. It's something I've come to realize.

Sunlight from the window pours through the sheer curtains, throwing muted light into the room. I turn the pendant over and over, watching it glint, watching the calla lily come and go.

To and fro.

To and fro.

And then,

I see her.

Olivia.

As clear as day,

Standing in front of me.

"Can you bring him to me?" she asks, her voice low and soft. "That's all I want to know."

Confusion billows like waves, through me, over me, around me.

Can I?

"I don't know," I tell her. "Where are you?"

I'm puzzled, but the vision ends with nausea, the way they always do.

When I become conscious again, I'm on my hands and knees on the floor, the room spinning to a stop around me.

As soon as I'm able, I stagger to my room and make a cup of Sabine's tea, because it calms me. It's the only thing that does.

At dinner, Dare is playing the piano, the notes wafting gently.

"Time here passes so quickly," I mention to Eleanor. I sip at another cup of tea, because it feels like that's all I do now. My hold on reality is tenuous, and all I can do is safeguard it.

Eleanor lifts an eyebrow but doesn't argue.

"Time is your enemy, Calla," is all she says. I set my cup down, and stare into it, and the tea leaves seem to have formed a question mark. I stare at it, mesmerized until Jones comes to take it away.

It's that night when I dream again.

But I don't dream of Olivia. I dream of my own mother, of Finn and my father, and of Dare.

The night is dark, the ground is cold.

That's what I'm thinking as we pile into our car, Finn and my father and me.

Someone is chasing us,
But that's impossible.
Because we live on top of a mountain,
And no one else is there.
My phone is in my lap.
My mother is screaming.
Dare is walking up the mountain, covered in blood.
Everything goes black.
I don't know.
I don't know.
I don't know.

I'm awake and I'm muttering and it's a minute before my words become coherent.

"The night is dark, the ground is cold."

I don't know what it means.

All I know is I'm the rabbit and Whitley is the hole and I'm fallingfallingfalling.

I'm terrified of the dark, because it seems to growl outside of my window.

I'm terrified of being alone, and so I bolt out of bed like a shot,

And make my way to Dare's bed.

I expect him to turn me away, but he doesn't.

He's in his sheets, twisted among blankets, but he doesn't act surprised to see me.

He simply opens his arms.

"Come here," he says,

so I do.

***

Sabine's voice lulls me, calms me.

"It's meant to be," she tells me, and I don't understand.

"What is?" I ask, and I sound so young, like a child. It's my innocence shining through and she smiles.

"Everything."

"Am I here for a reason?" I ask, although I already know the answer.

"Yes," she nods. "You are. And you'll come to it."

"Can you help?"

She nods again. "I already am, child. I already am."

She hands me tea and I take it.

"Is there valium in this?" I ask, only half joking and she smiles.

"No."

"Can there be?"

She smiles again. "You don't need it."

I beg to differ, but I don't.

"The truth is coming, child. Be ready for it."

I try to be, but it's hard, because I don't know what to watch for.

I go through the motions of my days, sitting with Eleanor when she asks, and spending my nights with Dare.

During the days, he's aloof and cool and detached, but at night, he's different.

He's warm and gentle and mine.

By night I am free.

Nocte liber sum.

Tonight, he waits for me.

Tonight, he lies next to me, propped on his elbow, staring down at me.

"You've always been mine," he tells me, his voice low. "Even before you knew it."

He kisses me almost before I can answer, before I can tell him that he's mine, too. I sigh and he sucks it in, his tongue in my mouth. His lips are soft, his arms are hard, and I don't want to ever leave this bed.

For the first time, I fall asleep in his arms, the rhythm of his breathing and his heart lulling me into sleep.

His arms can't keep the dreams away.

There's blood, like always, but it isn't mine.

It isn't Finn's.

It's Dare's.

Olivia stands in front of me again, her eyes accusatory.

Surprised, I stare at her.

"Why are you here?"

She stares back.

"Why are you? You don't belong with him."

"I do," I argue. *"I do."*

"You don't deserve him," she whispers, her face turning white. *"You're his downfall."*

"Why am I his downfall?" I almost scream it. *"I'm harmless. I haven't hurt a soul."*

"But you did," she argues simply, waving her arm. *The cliffs by my house appear, and my mom's smashed car is in the ravine. There's blood, there's screams and they're dead.*

"I called my mom," I remember. *"She crashed into my brother."*

Olivia stares at me. "The past is a prison, and you'll never break free."

"Wake up, Cal. Wake up."

It's Dare now, and he's murmuring into my ears and his grip is too hard on my arms. I squirm away.

"Why did you say that?" he demands, his eyes so stormy. The sheets are around his waist and his chest is bare.

"Say what?" I say dumbly, fighting to emerge from the cloud of sleep.

"The past is a prison," he answers harshly. "My mother used to say that."

I shake my head slowly from side to side. "I don't know why I said it."

I can't tell him that I'm dreaming of his mother.

He'll think I'm crazy,

because I am.

He pulls away from me and his absence is cold.

"What's going on, Calla?" he asks, his back to me as he sits on the side of the bed. "What do you know?"

I'm a terrible liar, so I decide not to try.

The consequences can be damned.

"I know that everyone wants an answer from me. I know I'm here for a reason."

Dare looks at me over his shoulder, and his expression is so vulnerable.

"I'm tired of feeling crazy," I tell him. "Is that the answer? Is that what everyone is waiting for? For me to admit that I'm crazy?"

He shakes his head and sighs.

"Are you lying to me?" I demand and he pushes my hair back with his fingers.

"No."

"A secret is the same thing as a lie," I tell him.

He looks away, because he knows.

Chapter Twenty-Seven

Day by day, I'm more and more convinced that I'm slipping away from sanity.

Day by day, Sabine convinces me that I'm not.

"Close your eyes," Sabine directs me, so I do. She takes my hand and hers is dry, it's small and twisted and I absorb her warmth.

"Picture the place where you saw Olivia," she tells me, so I do.

I hear the ocean, I see the pictures of Dare, I see her filmy nightgown, her soft heart-shaped face. I hear the accusation in her voice.

"Bring him to me," she directs me.

"Where are you?" I ask.

"I'm nearby," she answers mysteriously.

"Can you tell me?"

She shakes her head and her face is so very sad.

"No. You must figure it out."

I feel helpless and scared, and that feeling builds and builds.

"I can't figure it out," I tell her desperately. *"That's the problem. You're dead. I don't know where you are."*

"You can," she assures me. *"You must. Energy cannot be destroyed. I'm everywhere."*

I squeeze my eyes closed and when I do, the images shimmer and change.

I'm getting into a car.

Finn is with me, and my father, too.

"If I'm going, I'm driving," I tell them.

And I drive down the mountain.

And my mother,

My mother,

My mother.

The night is dark, the ground is cold.

The words whisper and morph and I'm confused.

I look at Olivia.

"That isn't what happened."

She nods and she's sad and her eyes become headlights.

I startle, and my eyes open.

Sabine is waiting for me, waiting for answers.

All I have are questions,

And confusion,

And lies.

It didn't happen that way.

Sabine is still waiting, her eyes dark.

"Did you see Olivia?"

I nod. Because I did see her.

"What was around her? The sea? Was there anything else?"

I shake my head.

"No. She was just standing in front of me."

Sabine clucks, and she's patient. "You must open your mind, Calla. Let it come."

I tried. But when I do, nonsense comes.

Lies.

But I nod, because what else can I do?

They need me to figure this out.

Olivia is lost.

And so am I.

This can't be real.

Dreams aren't real.

"*Your* dreams are," Sabine tells me. "Dreams are your mind's way of leading you to the light. Follow it, Calla."

The only thing I follow is Dare. He comes to get me and we walk the halls, and we stroll through the gardens and we make our way to our spot.

The secret garden,

Our place.

The angels stare at us with empty eyes, and I sag into Dare.

He's so warm,

So strong, so strong,

So real.

"Is this happening?" I ask him. "Because sometimes, I can't tell the difference."

He tilts my head back with his thumb, lifting my face to the sky. His eyes claim me, stroke me, ignite me.

I fold into his palms,

And he holds me up.

"I'm real," he says into my hair. "You're real."

We're standing in the sun,

There's no reason to be afraid.

Right?

Dare kisses me and his lips are sunlight. He touches me and his fingers are the moon. It's night somewhere, and by night we are free.

We come together like the stars,

Beneath the shelter of the gazebo.

Away from sight,

Away from everything.

Just us.

Our skin is hot,

Our mouths are needy.

We are alone.

But for the godforsaken angels.

The angels scare me," I whisper to Dare, and I clutch him close.

He holds me tight.

"I know," he says. "Why is that?"

"I don't know," I answer, and it's the truth. "Maybe it's their eyes. They see me."

"I see you," he reminds me, and his eyes are black.

Black, black,

Black as night.

"Will you always?" I murmur, and his neck tastes like salt. My fingers find his LIVE FREE.

"Yes," he promises.

"Repromissionem," I tell him. "It's Latin."

"I know."

Chapter Twenty-Eight

The kitchens are surprisingly bright and I pick at my bagel, perched on a stool as Sabine cooks.

"Aren't there cooks here?" I ask curiously, because I've never been in here before.

"Of course, child," she answers without turning around. "But I brew my own tea."

The pot she's stirring is large, and I eye it doubtfully.

"That's a big pot for tea, Sabine."

She laughs, then studies me.

"I want to read your cards again," she announces. When I'm instantly resistant, she adds. "One last time."

One last time?

Ok.

I follow her to her room, and she spreads my cards in a circle.

"Ah," she breathes, drawing a card. "The Knight of Pentacles." She looks up at me. It means

259

something is finally coming to fruition. It's almost time, child."

"What's almost time?"

She draws another card without answering.

She turns it around.

A woman holds scales, her face serene.

"Justice," Sabine says. "She represents balance. A balanced mind, a logical heart. Things will come together for you soon. You'll see things as they are."

God, I hope.

She bends her head and her fingers move, and she comes back up with one last card.

It's the dark skull.

The death card.

"What does that mean?" my voice is shaky, and I already know, of course.

She shakes her head. "It doesn't always mean death, child. Sometimes, it just means a shift in the order of things, or a rebirth, even."

"But sometimes… it just means death, right?"

My voice is small, and Sabine nods.

"And in this case?'

She shrugs. "I don't know. We'll have to wait and see."

It's not the answer I wanted.

I hesitate, but then my words come out before I can stop them.

"Do you know what happened to my uncle?"

Sabine stares at the table, without looking up.

"Do you know?" I ask gently.

"Just because you think you want the answer to something doesn't mean you actually do," she replies, her words a bit broken.

I stare her down.

She stares back, not intimidated. "Dare is a good boy," she insists, although I never said otherwise. "And what he did... well, it had to be done. He was young and he paid the price. He never deserved it."

But she won't say more, and I'm not sure I want to know.

I drift out of her room,

Toward the stables.

I can't be inside,

I can't be contained.

My thoughts are my enemy because they think about things I don't want to know.

I ask the groom to saddle Jupiter.

"Are you sure, Miss?" he looks at me, waiting for someone else to appear. "You want to ride alone?"

I nod. Of course I'm sure.

The breeze pushes my hair away from my face as I ride away from the house,

As I ride towards the pond.

The place Dare took me swimming.

I loop Jupiter's reins on a tree branch, and leave him eating clover.

I strip off my shirt and shorts, and wade into the water.

It's not as cold as it was before,

It doesn't take my breath away.

I slip under,

Allowing the water to cover my face, to cover my head, and my hair billows toward the surface. I stay under as long as I can, until my lungs are hot and heavy, then I kick to the surface. Pushing onto my back, I stare at the sky as I float.

I'm buoyant,

I'm a boat.

But then she's in front of me again.

Olivia.

Her hair is on fire and her eyes are wild.

"Help him!" she screeches.

I look to where she's pointing, but there's only a car, a smashed silver mess.

"You did this," she croons, rocking back and forth, sinking onto her heels. Her sheer nightgown drags in the water.

All of a sudden, the car catches fire, even though it's half submerged. It flares like a flash in a pan, and then the rest of it is underwater, extinguished.

A shadow flashes by.

The boy in the hood.

What does he want?

Then I yank myself out of the water,

And I'm back at Whitley.

I'm in the bathtub, the water spilling over the sides.

Dare has a washcloth in his hand, running it over my arms. I still his hand with my own, my voice wild.

"What happened? God, just tell me. I can't take this anymore, Dare."

He stares at me sadly, and the front of his shirt is wet.

His expression reminds me of his little boy face, the haunted one, the sad one. The one he had because my uncle beat him, and because his own mother let him.

"You're almost there, Calla-Lily. You're almost there."

His words are careful and slow, and I hesitate, because I'm afraid that *there* might just kill me.

Chapter Twenty-Nine

Days pass and they turn into nights, and all of them pass in Dare's arms. He holds me, croons to me, loves me.

And

Then

One

Day,

When the sky is blue and for once it isn't raining,

We take a trip to town.

Dare drives and we put the windows down, and the wind blows through our hair on the road.

I buy him a t-shirt because he doesn't own one.

Black, with orange letters.

Irony is Lost on You.

"But it's not," he chuckles when I hand it to him. "Life is ironic. It's not lost on me."

But he puts it on, right over his button-up and he looks ridiculous. He doesn't seem to mind, and he holds my hand in the daylight.

"Let's drive to the ocean."

"Ok." Because I miss it. Because even though Oregon is rainy and gray, I loved living next to the water.

As we walk to the car, I'm distracted by a street vendor, a tiny old man with blue eyes and a friendly grin. He has jewelry laid out on a cart, and something catches my eye.

A silver ring, gleaming in the light.

"All of my things are antiques," he tells me proudly. I pick up the ring.

"That's a size twelve. It was the wedding ring of an aristocrat," he explains. "I buffed the scratches out, but that ring is loved. His wife swore to me it protected him, on more than one occasion."

"Protected him from what?" I ask curiously. The old man smiles.

"From everything."

I buy it on the spot, and offer it to Dare.

"Everyone can use protection," I tell him, half-joking, half not. He rolls his eyes but slides it on to his middle finger.

"Then I shall be protected," he announces. "I'll consider it an early Valentine's Day gift.

"Valentine's is months away," I point out. He smiles.

"I know."

I feel an overwhelming sense of déjà vu, as though I know what is going to happen next… as though all of this already happened. Didn't it?

I don't know.

I don't know anything at all.

It's the strangest, most frustrating feeling in the world. I try to ignore it.

We pile into the car, and Dare's hand is on my leg, his fingers curled around my thigh. He's warm, and I absorb it, and I lay my head back on the seat, warming up in the sun.

I wake up to the sound of the waves.

"You fell asleep," Dare says, and he's watching me sleep. "I thought you needed to rest."

The sun has gone down a bit, and the breeze is chilly, so while we walk on the shore, Dare wraps his arm around my shoulders, hugging me into his side.

"I feel like home here," I confide, as I watch the gray water break on the sand.

"Then we should've come here sooner," he says, and his fingers are light on my skin.

The dying light glimmers on the water and for a minute, it looks like flame.

And that minute, that one minute,

Is

All

It

Takes.

Things crash into me, one after the other.

Everything is on fire.

Through the flames, I see Dare.

He's shouting,

He's afraid.

"I…" my voice is aghast and I see it in my head. Everything.

I see everything.

I see what happened, but I can't tell the memories from the visions.

Everything is overwhelming,

The emotions,

The memories,

The fear.

In a flash, I see years.

Year of memories.

Dare and Finn and I playing when we were small,

Mud pies, and swimming in the pond, and summers in England.

I see Olivia, because I knew her.

Long black hair, big dark eyes.

Eyes like Dare's.

Her whispers were always so soft.

"You can't be together," she'd told us. "It isn't right. It's not right. You know he can't leave here."

Dare can't leave Whitley.

He can't leave.

He can't leave.

But he did.

I see it.

He came to get me because I lost everything.

And when we arrive here at Whitley, he lost everything too.

I see him with his mother in his arms,
Through the flames of a fire.
"Help!" he shouts.   And Olivia is limp and dead.
"Help!"
But no one could.
Because an accident is an accident is an accident.
"Was it an accident?" I ask limply as we stand in
the crypts next to her name.
"You know it wasn't," Dare tells me, his voice so
rigid and hard.   "We drove her to it.   It was us.   It was
us."
I see Olivia screaming.
"You took him from me.   He wasn't yours to take.
He's not yours, he's mine."
In her eyes, I see madness.
I recognize it.
She's the rabbit and I'm the rabbit and we're both
crazy.
I see her taillights leaving the house,
I see the fire.
I see Dare.

I open my eyes, and it's painful.

"Your mother drove off the Seven Sisters cliffs
because of us."

Dare's eyes contain things I've never seen before,
levels of unthinkable sadness.   He nods.

"Yes."

"You think it's my fault."   My words scrape my
throat and I feel desperate.

"No."

"You lost your mom and I lost mine, and they were two separate nights. Two separate things."

I hear the desperation in my voice because I can't keep anything straight. All of my memories swirl together and nothing makes sense.

Dare nods. "They were two separate accidents. Two separate nights."

"But your mother's wasn't an accident." I point this out thinly, and again he nods.

"Our family is cursed. Because we have to pay for the sins of our fathers," I say in confusion, remembering Sabine's words. "Everyone is dead and this doesn't make sense."

I can't wrap my head around it. Any of it. Because my father never committed a sin. Sabine is wrong about that.

But Dare's mother is still dead.

"Take me to the cliffs," I tell Dare. "I've got to see it. I've got to understand."

He doesn't want to, but he does. He drives me and I'm panicky, and as we climb the twisted road, I can't breathe.

And then he's there.

The boy in the hood.

Standing in front of our car, he cocks his head.

"He's been waiting for me," I realize aloud. "He's been here for me all along."

Dare stares at me confused and I cry out to stop the car, so he does.

I leap out and I chase the boy, straight toward the top, until I'm on the edge of the world and all I can hear is the ocean.

It growls at me.

It roars.

The boy shimmers in the night, a memory that I can't grab. My mind flickers and wavers and wanes.

"Come back!" I shout and the wind catches my words and carries them away. "I need to know what you know!"

I've been here before, I think.

I've been here before.

The wind,

The water,

The panic.

I hear Dare calling out for me, but I don't stop.

I can't.

I chase the boy, but he's been chasing me all along.

He knows the secret.

He knows.

He knows.

He looks back but I can't see his face and I race toward him, hurtling myself, lunging, my fingers stretching.

And then I'm falling,

Falling,

Falling,

And the water is cold,

The sand is damp.

And I'm broken,

I'm broken,

I'm broken.

Dare is with me, and there's blood all over his shirt.

"Are you ok?" he asks quickly, and his hands are on mine. "God, Calla, are you ok? Open your eyes, open your eyes."

Finn and my mother and my father are all spread on the sand. But that was a different night.

This is my night.

Not theirs.

They died already.

Time spins and I'm in the sand with Dare, and I'm in his lap, and the foam covers us both, and the water is bloody, and the blood is mine.

"Do you see?" he asks quietly, his new ring glinting in the light, because he's protected now, but I'm not.

"Yes," I murmur.

Protect me, St. Michael.

Pray for me.

Pray for me.

My memories.

"My memories weren't real," I tell myself, and I already knew that to be true. But I didn't know the truth.

They were always a jumbled up mess.

They weren't completely real.

But they are now.

Painfully,

Nightmarishly,

Real.

I play it again in my head,

Again,

And again,

And again.

"My friend had to cancel," Finn scowls. "So I guess I've been stood up. Are you sure you don't want to come?"

Ugh. I groan internally because I'm not a fan of Quid Pro Quo, but Finn has been looking forward to this concert for months. I'm just about to agree to going, when my father walks in.

"I'll go. I don't want you going into the city alone this late."

"Sa-weet!" Finn crows, and I don't point out that most boys would rather die than go to a concert with their father. He's not 'most boys' and we know it.

My father puts his hand on my shoulder.

"Hey, I know what," he suggests. "I want you to come too. I don't want you here alone. Not tonight. You're coming too, Calla. I'll buy your ticket."

"Heck yeah," Finn *says, and I want to scream,*
Noooooo. Don't.

Because this is a memory and it's real and I can't
change it.

We pile into the car,
And I can't stop.
I can't stop.
I'm going to kill them,
And I can't stop.
Our car barrels down the mountain.
And my mom forgot her glasses.
I can't change it now.
The night is shattered by screams.
Because I hit my mother and they're all dead.

"My family is all dead. My father, my brother,
my Finn. And your mother is dead too, and it's all our
fault."

My words are finally true. And I see things.

I see things.

I see things.

Dare nods, and his movement is sad and I'm
gurgling. I can't breathe and my teeth are red.

"Have you known this whole time?" I ask,
because I didn't. Because I'm so fucked up that my
mind has created stories out of stories out of stories.

He nods. "Yeah. But you didn't."

He looks away and for a second, I think that's all,
That's all there is to know,
That's the last of the secrets.

But his face is hurt,

And pained,

And I know in my heart... it's not.

There's something else.

There's

One

More

Thing.

My lungs are hot and red and bloody, and my throat is constrained. I can barely move and the pain,

The pain,

The pain.

I can't breathe.

"Tell me," I murmur. "I'm ready. Tell me the last secret."

Dare picks up my hand and there's a shadow behind him,

The hooded boy.

Of course.

He's been waiting for me,

following me,

he's been here for me all along.

Standing at Dare's shoulder, he turns his face,

And I can finally see it.

It's black as night,

And he has no eyes.

I gasp, because I finally know who he is.

He's Death.

I saw him on Sabine's tarot card.

Dare's words grow quieter and I strain to hear, because he's talking through a tunnel, through light and wind and my heartbeat.

"You're dying," he whispers. "If you don't wake up, you'll be lost."

Chapter Thirty

The world slows to a stop.

My heart beats.

It's dark.

There is no ocean.

There are no waves.

There is no sun or rain or moon.

There is only my breathing, and beeps, and fingers wrapped around my hand, and I'm in a bed. I'm not in the ocean or the on the cliffs.

"Come back to me, Calla," Dare whispers, and angst laces his words, and his words impale my heart. "Please God, come back to me. Time is running out. Don't do this, please, God, don't do this. They're going to take you off the machine, and if you don't breathe on your own, you'll die. Please God. Please."

He begs someone, whether it is God or me, I don't know.

"We've already lost everything else," he whispers. "Please, God. Come back to me. Come home to me. Come home."

I try to open my eyes, but it's too hard.

My eyelids are heavy.

The darkness is black.

Dare keeps talking, his words slow and soothing and I might float away on them. It would be so easy.

Death waits for me.

I can see his face now, and he waits in the light behind Dare's shoulder.

He nods.

It's time.

But it can't be. Because Dare is here, and still holding my hand. He talks to me, he tells me everything that's happened, and when he gets tired of talking, he hums.

The same wordless, tuneless song I've been hearing all along.

Death moves closer, one step nearer.

I try to cry out, but nothing comes.

I try again to open my eyes, but I can't. And I can't move my fingers.

It's all too much.

Too much.

I think about getting frantic,

And I almost do.

But to keep calm,

I replay the facts in my head.

My name is Calla Price.

I'm eighteen years old, and I'm half of a whole.

My other half, my twin brother, my Finn, is crazy.

Finn is dead.

My mother is dead.

My father is dead.

Dare's mother is dead.

I've spent every summer at Whitley my entire life.

I've loved Dare since I was small.

I've been floating in a sea of insanity, and I can't wake up.

I can't wake up.

Dare is my lifeline.

He's still here.

I focus every ounce of strength I have, trying to force my hand into gripping his, the hands that I love so much, the hand that has held mine for so long.

But I'm helpless.

I'm weak.

Death takes another step, but I can't scream.

It's when he touches Dare that I bolster my strength.

He puts his hand on Dare's shoulder,

And I can't take that.

Don't touch Dare, I want to scream. *You took his mother, but you're not taking* him*! He's innocentHe'sInnocentHe'sInnocent!*

But his fingers drum on Dare's skin,

And everything in me boils,

And screams.

And somehow,

Some way,

I harness my energy,

And my finger twitches.

Dare's humming stops.

"Calla?" he asks quickly, hope so potent in his voice.

I move my finger again, and it's all the strength I have left.

I can't move again, but I think it was enough.

Dare's gone,

Gone from my side,

Yelling for someone,

For anyone.

Other voices fill my room,

Circling my bed,

And Dare's voice is drowned.

He's gone,

but others have replaced him.

I'm poked,

I'm prodded,

My lids are lifted and lights are shined into my eyes.

"It's a miracle," someone announces.

I can't stay awake.

My strength is gone.

I fall asleep wishing Dare would come back.

I don't know how long I sleep.

I only know that I dream,

And now, when I dream,

They're lucid.

I'm no longer insane.

I don't know why.

Olivia sits in front of me, her smile gentle and soft.

"My boy wasn't meant for you, but you took him anyway."

I swallow hard because I did take him.

"You have to know that's the way of things," I offer. "Boys can't stay with their mothers forever. It wasn't my fault you died."

"I killed myself," she says simply. "I didn't mean to, but I couldn't take any more pain."

I understand pain.

I nod.

"My brother...."

My voice trails off. Thinking about Finn makes my chest hurt.

"I can't live without my Finn," I say limply. And Olivia shakes her head.

"You have to. He's gone, but you're not."

"Why did I keep dreaming about you?" I ask her, confused now in a very real way.

She gets up and her form is so slight, so small. She's dark like Dare and her eyes gleam like the night.

Black, black eyes that examine my soul.

She cocks her head, in the same way that Dare does.

"Because you couldn't remember me. You couldn't remember what happened. And what happened to me, is why Dare is who he is. He's a

protector, Calla. He'll protect you until his dying day."

"Why did you want me to bring him to you?" I ask. "You're dead."

"Because I left him and I shouldn't have," she says, closing her dark eyes. "He didn't deserve it. And now he's in pain, and he'll stand by you until he can't stand up anymore."

She's right.

Despite his own pain, he was by my bed,

He's been here the whole time,

humming to me.

She shakes her head. "My son had to do what he did," she tells me, and I know she's talking about Richard now. "I wasn't strong enough to stop it, but he was. Dare was strong enough."

Her voice is small.

"Your story is so sad," I tell her, because it is. The saddest thing I've ever heard. She shakes her head knowingly.

"It's not. The saddest thing is knowing that you think none of this has been real. Your dreams are always real, Calla. Even if you don't realize it. You've got to open your eyes. Open your eyes.

Open your eyes.

Open your eyes."

I startle awake, the insistence of her voice shocking me into lucidity.

My eyes open.

The light is so bright it's blinding.

The humming stops.

"Calla?" The voice is familiar. It's a voice I love, more than life, more than anything.

Finn.

He grips my hand and little

by

little,

My eyes adjust and I can see him.

I focus on his face, on the haphazard curls that frame his face like a halo, the pale blue eyes and the freckle on his hand.

"Calla, you're awake," he says in wonder, so much surprise in his voice. "I thought… God, it doesn't matter what I thought."

He thought I was going to die.

Because I was going to.

And he *is* dead,

And I've got to stop imagining him. I blink hard, holding my eyes closed.

I try to speak, but my voice won't come, my throat far too dry. There's a tube down my throat, I realize groggily. I pull at it with my hand, but someone stops me.

I open my eyes to find a blonde nurse.

My eyes widen when I see her nametag.

Ashley.

The Ashley from my dreams, only now she's not a girl in an evening gown anymore, she's a nurse in puppy dog scrubs. She smiles when she sees my eyes open, and she mills about my bed.

"Don't fret," she tells me. "I've called the doctor and she'll be right in. For now, close your eyes and I'll get this tube out. I'm going to count to three, then I want you to exhale."

I do, and on three, she pulls the tube out of my throat.

It feels like a snake in the grass, slithering away, and I've never been so happy to see something go.

My hands flutter to my throat, cupping it, and Finn holds a straw to my lips.

"Drink this," he tells me, so I do. I feel like I haven't had a drink in a hundred years, and so I drink, and drink, and drink, even though it hurts to swallow.

When I'm finished, I clear my throat.

My words are dry, but I'm able to speak them.

"I'm so sorry, Finn."

There's pain on his face, real pain, and he closes his eyes for a minute.

"It was an accident," he finally says. "It wasn't your fault."

But it was.

I know it, and so does he.

"What happened to me?"

All I remember is standing on the cliffs,

Then falling.

Finn looks away, his blue eyes pained.

"You weren't in your right mind. You chased something over the cliffs."

I'm astounded, frozen. "I jumped off the cliffs?"

The boy in the hood.

I remember now, and my eyes grow wide.

"You've had a mental break, Calla. You were supposed to be recovering at Whitley, recovering from losing us. But a lot happened, and your mind just couldn't bend any more."

My chest feels shaky as I breathe, and I look around my hospital room. Two chairs, a table, a clock. A dry erase board that reads *Your nurse today will be Ashley*. A stack of books, a pillow, a blanket.

Dare isn't here.

I miss him.

I need him.

He pulled me from the insanity. I know that much is true.

My mind played trick after trick after trick, but Dare stuck by me until the end.

I take another drink, and glance at the clock.

5:35.

Finn talks to me, about dad, about mom, about the funerals, about life.

"And the priest." Finn pauses. "A priest took you under his wing. He was here to visit you several times."

I blink.

"Was his name Father Thomas?"

Finn nods slowly. "How did you... never mind. He came to visit you a lot. The last time he... he gave you the Last Rites, Calla." His voice breaks off and he looks away.

Through this holy anointing may the Lord in his love and mercy help you with the grace of the Holy Spirit. May the Lord who frees you from sin save you and raise you up.

I remember.

They all thought I was going to die.

Did Dare?

6:02.

Ashley comes back to say that the doctor had been delayed, but she'd be here soon.

Finn chats aimlessly, and I listen, but not really.

6:25.

The door opens, and my heart leaps, thinking it's Dare.

It's not.

It's Sabine.

Only it's not.

"I'm Dr. Andros," she tells me in a throaty voice, a familiar voice, a voice I've heard for months. I thought it was in my dreams, but it was real. "And you gave us quite a scare."

She pokes at me with small hands, and I marvel at how much she is like Sabine, at how interesting our brains are when they are traumatized.

"You're going to make a full recovery," she tells me finally, and she looks a bit astonished.

"Thank you," I tell her. And the teas she gave me in my dreams must've been medication in real life, sedatives. She nods and she's gone.

I'm left alone with Finn, and it's 6:42.

I don't want to make him feel *less than,*

But I'm dying to see Dare.

Every molecule and fiber of my being needs to see him.

6:43.

So I have to ask.

"Finn, when will Dare be coming?"

Finn is at the window, and when he turns, his eyes are clouded in something dark, something hesitant. He stares at me, wondering what he should say, intent on handling me carefully.

We have to handle her carefully.

I remember the words from before, when I couldn't see who spoke them.

A weight,

a heavy,

heavy

weight,

settles in my stomach because Finn is so very careful, because he doesn't know what to say.

Fear flutters through me, and I move my tongue.

"Finn," I say again, and horror is forming in my heart. "When will Dare get here?"

My fear takes off like birds, because Finn shakes his head.

He sits down, and picks up my hand.

His fingers are cold.

His body is still.

My heart is a weight,

dropping through my chest,

breaking all my bones.

"Calla," Finn says carefully, his blue eyes trained on my face. "Dare is…"

His jagged voice breaks off,

like pieces of shattered glass.

I squeeze his hand,

As hard as I can.

Because I think I already know the answer.

To be continued…

In the third and final book of the Nocte Trilogy,

LUX.

About the Author

Courtney Cole is a New York Times and USA Today bestselling author who collects dashboard hula girls, is in love with LOVE, and writes beneath palm trees. She lives in sunny Florida with her family and is constantly daydreaming new stories. To learn more about her, please visit www.courtneycolewrites.com

2625

Made in the USA
Lexington, KY
03 February 2015